TOM
WYATT

AN OLD DOG WITH THREE TALES

A collection of three
Short Stories
with a twist

First published April 2021

This book is dedicated to my long suffering
wife Mo, who puts up with me whiling
away long winter nights two-finger
typing on the kitchen table

1

A Reciprocal Arrangement

Freda and Joe want something new in their lives and get more than they bargained for.

Chapter 1

Freda

Freda Turnbull was bored.

She reflected upon her life as she stood at the sink, washing by hand the last few items of crockery that wouldn't fit into the overflowing dishwasher.

Staring out of the window she mentally broke down her day – *every* day – into its component parts in an effort to decide what she could change, how she could perhaps add a little excitement to her humdrum existence:

Up at 7 am, light the fire in the snug, make breakfast for 8 o'clock, call upstairs to Joe, her husband asking if he was ready for his egg to be fried. Wash up, make the bed, phone her daughter for ten minutes before putting the washing machine on.

Prepare something to cook for lunch, take a coffee and piece of cake down to the shed for Joe, hang out the washing, then lunch itself, bake another cake, etc., etc. *ad infinitum*. It was always the same, every day.

She thought about her husband Joe. How he'd changed over the years, from being an attractive, active, even exciting partner into the quiet, remote, rather nondescript soul that now spent three quarters of his waking hours in the shed at the bottom of the garden. Then, regular as clockwork, he would come in at four and sit in his armchair, to read the paper and watch the endless supply of mind-numbing quiz shows on the television or occasionally doze off.

They rarely spoke. The only words to pass between them were niceties like 'Did you sleep well?' or 'That was a nice lunch, dear,' or 'How's that knee of yours healing?' after she'd scraped it when she fell with an armful of washing on the back step.

There was never any real cosy chat or topic of mutual interest to discuss.

She remembered how things used to be when they first married in 1962. At bedtime neither of them could wait to get upstairs and get on with things under the eiderdown. But now here she was in 1990 going to bed at separate times. Separate beds. He would hang back.

'I'll just finish watching this last programme and be up in a minute,' he would say.

'Well, I'm tired so don't wake me when you come up,' she would reply.

It had been like that really since the children had flown the nest. That was 8 years ago. Here she was at the ripe old age of fifty six - middle aged she thought, still looking fairly good, slimmish with no sagging flesh, no bingo wings, hair still its natural mousy colour. She was no great beauty, she knew that, but she wasn't ugly either.

What could she do to improve the rest of her life?

'Something might come along,' she said to herself as she ran the dishcloth over the worktop one final time and took off her rubber gloves.

Chapter 2

Joe

Joe Turnbull stared at the piece of wood in the vice, wondering how he could repair the split where he had accidentally damaged the wood as he miss-hit the nail with his claw hammer.

His shed was small – too small, largely because it had to contain the garden tools, lawnmower and of course, the garden furniture when the weather turned inclement.

Room for his projects was at a premium and his ability to work neatly was frustrated by the lack of space.

But then, it didn't really matter, for his projects generally came to nothing. His satisfaction was gained mainly from being there, fiddling, whiling away his time.

Since his early retirement from bus driving for the local depot, he'd found that working in his shed was so much better than hanging around the house, being disturbed by the vacuum cleaning or being asked to help fold the newly washed bed-linen or listening to Freda gabbling on about things. For example: how the lout living next door would spend hours kicking his football up against their garage door, the constant din driving her to distraction. She had a list of favourite rants. He was sick of hearing them.

'Shall we go for a walk?' he used to ask.

'No, you know walking gives me problems with my back,' she'd reply, 'besides, I've got the carpets to hoover and the shopping to do.'

So Joe would go back to his shed.

Joe smoked a pipe, but not everywhere. Freda didn't like the smell, so the shed was about the only place where he could smoke in peace. It also helped him think. Whenever he had a problem that he couldn't immediately resolve, he would take out his *Clan* tobacco, clean out his pipe and refill it, then light up. Relaxing in the tatty, threadbare armchair in the corner he would puff away gently, turning over the problem in his mind, eventually coming up with a solution.

But today, staring at his piece of wood, his problem took a different form. It was proving far more taxing. Though he was staring at it, he was not thinking about the repair but about how he could get out of this boring life of his, even if it was with Freda, although that would not necessarily be his preferred option.

'I'm nearly sixty-one. Can I put up with this for the next twenty years?' he asked himself.

He had no answer to his question though. At least, not yet.

'Never mind, I'll think of something,' he whispered.

He looked at his watch. Nearly four o'clock. Soon be time for a cuppa and the paper, he thought.

Chapter 3

Margaret (Maggie)

It was Tuesday. Freda called in at the butchers looking for bacon scraps and a pound of chuck steak for a pie.

Margaret Hough was ahead of her in the queue, and Freda called out to her.

'Maggie, how's your boy's chicken pox today?'

Maggie looked round, waved with a smile and moved out of her position at number 3 in the queue to stand beside Freda at number 6, which therefore became number 5.

'The spots are going and the doctor says he's not contagious no more,' she replied, 'but he's not going back to school 'till next week, just in case.'

Freda admired Maggie. She was only a few years younger, yet she was always so in control, always stood her corner, always ready to do something new, nothing seemed to phase her. She'd go climbing the fells with her husband Pete, swimming in the river, or out for picnics with the boys and Pete would even take her to the pictures once in a while.

Joe did none of those things.

Freda would ask 'Shall we go on holiday somewhere this year?' and Joe would reply:

'I don't see the point in paying all that money to a travel agent just to get disappointed when we get there – much better to stay at home, I would say.'

Maggie went on holiday every year, sometimes twice. Her life was exciting, Freda thought.

'I'm going line dancing tonight.' Maggie said, nudging Freda with her arm and winking.

'What the hell's that?' Freda asked.

'Don't know yet – never done it, but that new American woman that's moved in opposite us has booked the village hall and is starting a line dancing club, so I thought I'd give it a go. Hey! Why don't you come along too?'

Freda looked sheepish. 'Oh I don't think I'd be any good at dancing – if that's what it is. Joe always said I had two left feet, so we never did any.'

'Oh, don't be daft, just come along, it'll be fun. Tell you what, I'll call for you tonight at seven o'clock and we'll go together.'

At four o'clock that afternoon, when Joe arrived to read his paper, Freda announced that he'd be having his high tea earlier than usual. Five o'clock, she said.

''Cos tonight I'm going line dancing with that Maggie down the road, she's picking me up at seven.'

'What's that?' Joe enquired. 'If dancing's involved I don't think that's your type of thing – you never could before, so why try now?'

'I don't care – it'll just be a chance to do something different. And if I don't like it or I can't do it, I can always stop.'

'I suppose it's up to you.' Joe replied resignedly and closed the conversation by burying his head in his newspaper.

Freda, totally frustrated, stood staring at him for a few moments then marched back into the kitchen.

At six o'clock, Freda went upstairs to prepare for her outing. She took off her pinafore and sat down in front of the mirror at her dressing table.

Should she put on some make-up, she wondered. She rarely wore it and when she did she always felt she looked a bit tarty.

Perhaps just a little eye shadow and a smidgen of lipstick, she thought – and maybe a touch of rouge?

She went to her wardrobe and selected her best skirt and a plain navy jumper.

Looking at herself in the full-length mirror in the bathroom, she thought she looked a bit younger with make-up, and smiled at her reflection.

Satisfied that she was now ready for the occasion, she went down to Joe.

'How do I look, Joe?' She asked.

Joe turned his attention away from the television to squint sideways at Freda.

'Mutton dressed as lamb, I'd say,' he replied, then to soften his remark, 'only joking – you look OK I suppose, perhaps a touch too much make-up in my humble opinion.' Then changing the subject, he added: 'I might go down to the pub while you're out.'

Freda felt a little hurt by his comment, even though she knew it was par for the course these days.

'But you never go down the pub,' she said.

'No, but I thought I might do something different too – like you.'

Maggie turned up dead on the dot of seven o'clock. She laughed her socks off when she saw Freda.

'You can't go line dancing dressed like that love, you need jeans for line dancing apparently and you've got to have a Stetson.'

'What's that?' Freda asked.

'It's a hat like cowboys wear. I had a word with that American lady – Marlene, her name is – she said jeans are best and we can get the hat later if we don't have one.'

'But I don't have any jeans.'

'Well I s'pose it won't matter for the first time anyway,' Maggie replied, 'so let's go then.'

Chapter 4

Dorothy

Joe picked up his pipe and tobacco and went into the hall to fetch his flat-cap and windcheater.
Checking that the back door was locked, he then let himself out of the front door, pulled on the knocker until he heard the *Yale* latch click home into its keep, and set off for the King's Arms.

It had been a while since he last called in. He'd not know anyone by now, he thought, especially as it was now under new management. But for some reason he really fancied a pint of mild and couldn't get it out of his mind. So he marched down the road with more determination than usual.

Inside, the pub had changed considerably. The old velour wall benches had gone and all the small round tables had been replaced with square ones, a cruet set and menus placed carefully in the middle, and four chairs around each one.
The walls were now painted grey instead of the old flocked wallpaper, the red, heavily patterned *Axminster* carpet replaced with wooden flooring and the bar was now twice as long as before, with bar stools all along it.
The pub was full and people were eating. Not crisps, pickled eggs and pork scratchings like before, but proper food like scampi or pie and chips – stuff like that. Joe couldn't believe it.

He walked up to the bar and was greeted by a rather well endowed, dark-haired woman with a low-cut, black jumper and lots of cheap jewellery. Her fingernails were beautifully painted a bright red, he noticed, with tiny silver stars stuck all over them. She looked about fifty he thought, though the way she was dressed and made up, with her boobs almost hanging out of her jumper, she probably was a little younger.

'What can I get you, stranger?' she asked with a broad smile which displayed a mouthful of even, extremely white teeth.

Joe ordered a pint of mild.

'This place has changed a lot since I was last in here,' he said.

'That must have been a long time ago,' she replied, 'it's been like this since I first came, and that's four years ago.'

'So you're not the landlady then?'

She laughed. 'Good God, no, I wouldn't be daft enough to want to own a pub – too much hassle. I just work here two evenings a week, Tuesday and Thursday. I'm Dorothy – Dot to my pals,' she said, 'do you live around here then?'

'Just down the road, about a couple of hundred yards. The name's Joe by the way'

'On your own then Joe?'

'No, my other half's gone line dancing tonight and I just fancied a pint for a change.'

'Never done any of that,' she replied, 'though I've seen it on the telly. Looks a bit boring if you ask me. I prefer proper dancing, where you can get to grips with your partner. Used to go to the tea dances down at the Castle Hotel, but of course that's all shut now.'

She passed Joe's pint of mild across the bar and placed it on the towelling mat.

'On the house,' she said, 'but keep mum.' She tapped the side of her nose.

Joe picked it up and with a 'Cheers', took his first sip.

'I used to love dancing,' he started, 'but the wife was useless at it. We'd go down to the old Palais in town, but she'd always end up sitting it out and I'd be looking for someone to partner. 'Course, that's gone too now.'

'Do you still fancy it – dancing I mean?' Dorothy asked, laughing at her unintended innuendo.

Joe looked down at her enticing expanse of bare chest. 'To tell you the truth, I do miss it,' he said.

Dot noticed his stare and leaned over the bar pushing a few extra centimetres of flesh out of her jumper. 'Why don't we pair up and look for another dance-hall or something, somewhere?'

While he was considering her idea, Dot moved down the bar, distracted by another customer.

Joe took out his pipe, stuffed it with his *Clan* tobacco and lit up while she pulled the newcomer a pint of cider.

'Ooh! I do love the smell of that tobacco Joe,' she exclaimed on her return, 'reminds me of my old man. He used to smoke *Clan* too.'

'So has he given up now then?'

'I suppose in a way he has,' she said, 'he died four years ago. Got blown off a roof he was working on at the Electricity Board during a storm. Been on my own ever since. That's why I'm working here. His pension wasn't enough to keep me and a few extra bob here and there makes all the difference.'

'I'm sorry to hear that, Dot. You have my sympathy.'

'Oh, it's all right now. We weren't exactly a loving couple. Once we got married things fell apart a bit. Anyway, it was long enough ago for me to be over it now. But getting back to what we were saying, what do you think about my suggestion?'

'Well, it sounds ok, but I'm not sure the wife would feel the same about it – me with another woman an' all that.'

'But we'd only be dancing, wouldn't we?'

Joe guessed where she was going and left the question hanging in the air.

'It would have to be no more than once a week though,' he replied.

'Well, if your wife gets to like line dancing, we could do it the same night. That way it wouldn't get in the way of her life.'

'OK so when do we start and where do we go?'

'Well, I think before we start going to a dance hall, we'd better see how we get on, because we haven't danced together before. How about we have our first practice session at my place next week? I've got a stereo and lots of records.'

Chapter 5

Rufus

The village hall was bustling when Freda and Maggie arrived. There were around twenty five people enrolling for the line dancing at five pounds each and the atmosphere was a mixture of excitement and trepidation. Poor Freda was the only one without jeans, but by now she didn't care. She was just pleased to be doing something new – something different from her normal, boring regime.

With the American woman, Marlene, every one was labelled either a 'gal' or a 'guy', irrespective of age. And the age gap was huge. Some of the 'gals' were as young as eighteen or so, others as old as seventy but most of the 'guys' were around retirement age.

'OK guys and gals', Marlene chirped, 'I want you to form two lines, here and here' – she pointed to two places on the floor. 'I think you could line up alternate guy and gal, but there ain't enough guys, so the end of the line will be all gals. OK?'
Everyone duly obliged.
'I'm gonna start the music and I want you to watch my steps, then we'll all try it, OK?'

Freda was next to a 'guy' and a 'gal'. She looked at the 'guy' to her left, just at the same moment as he was appraising her. Their eyes met. He was tall with a bushy set of sideburns but his Stetson covered what hair he had. He had bright blue eyes and the nicest smile she had ever encountered on a man.

'Howdy,' he said, 'that's the right word isn't it?'

She laughed, 'Only if you're a Yankee,' she replied with a smile.

'No, I'm just trying to get in the mood.' he replied.

'I'm Freda,' she blurted, reddening slightly, 'what's your name?'

'Rufus...Rufus Williams.'

Sort of a dog's name, that, Freda thought.

'Have you done any of this before?' She asked

'Nope! First time, but I've been to the States, seen it there. That's where I got this hat.'

The conversation broke off as Marlene started the music.

'OK, guys and gals, these are the steps I want you to follow. They are pretty simple for this first lesson, but each week we will be getting a little more complex. By the time the ten lessons are over you will all become real good at it and be able to line-dance to anything with anybody. Here we go...'

And she stomped out a series of steps, calling out each one as she did so:

'Left foot forward, right to the left, left foot back and right to the side, turn ninety degrees to the right, then repeat...'

Soon everybody was doing it in unison and the hall floor shook to the rhythm of their boots. The noise was enough to distract the painting class next door, the majority of whom came to watch the spectacle.

Chapter 6

Joe and Dorothy

Joe was home by the time Freda got back from her line dancing. It was late, about eleven o'clock.

'You've been a long time,' said Joe, 'you must be out of breath by now.'

'Well, I was a bit, earlier on, but then Maggie said why not stay and have a cuppa and a biscuit, as most of them were. So I did.'

'Did you enjoy it?'

'Yes, I did actually. But I need to buy a pair of jeans though, for next week. I was the only 'gal' in a skirt.'

'Oh! So you're carrying on with it then?'

'Oh yes, it's quite good fun and good exercise too. It'll be good for me.'

She thought about Rufus. Would she be able to wait that long to see him again – he seemed such a nice, interesting man.

Joe was inwardly pleased that Freda had taken a liking to her line dancing, for it meant that he would be able to have another pint at the pub and continue his plans with Dorothy. He kept picturing himself dancing with her, up close, with that magnificent chest of hers pressing against his shirt. He felt weak at the knees just thinking about it. This was the beginning of a big change in his life, he thought.

And of course, he didn't have to wait 'till the following week. She worked at the pub on a Thursday as well, so he would have to find some excuse to have another pint then.

'What about you? Did you enjoy your pint?' Freda asked.

'As a matter of fact I did,' he replied, 'although the pub has changed a bit, and not for the better, I might add.'

'So will it become a regular occurrence?' Freda asked, hoping the answer would be a 'yes'.

'Well I don't see why not, although I might try a different day occasionally, just to see if there's a better crowd of people in there. I might go again on Thursday perhaps.'

'Well, I won't be coming with you,' she replied, 'all that smoke and the stale smell of toilets.'

'It's not like that now, Freda, but you can still smoke in there, so not your cup of tea, I know.'

Joe was pleased about that. And now he was free to go on Thursday.

Thursday arrived, although only slowly for Joe. At seven o'clock he rushed upstairs to have a quick wash and brush-up. He checked the stubble on his jaw – no need to shave, he thought, but he splashed on a drop of *Old Spice* to freshen up.

'I'm off now love,' he called from the hall as he put on his windcheater. 'See you later.'

Freda came out of the kitchen to see him off.

'You smell nice,' she said.

'Well, I didn't have time for a proper wash,' he stammered, trying not to look guilty, 'and I didn't want to stink too much, so I put a little after-shave on.'

'Pity you don't use it more often,' she scolded.

Having got away with that little fib, he set off at a fast pace for the pub. He promised to be there for seven thirty, but he was running a bit late. All the way there he had this vision of Dorothy with her low-cut jumper and heavily-contoured cleavage leaning over the bar in front of him.

He was disappointed then, to arrive and find no sign of her. Instead, there was a rather large, fat bloke in a red check shirt, sleeves rolled up revealing loads of tattoos, pulling the pints and laughing with the punters at the bar.

Joe ordered his own pint and went over to one of the square tables to sit down.

All of a sudden he felt he shouldn't be there. There was no need. He hadn't come down here for the drink, it was solely the draw of Dorothy. He felt totally dejected. Should he leave it and go home? He wondered. 'No, perhaps I should wait a while longer, she may be a little late.'

There was a menu on the table. He picked it up and idly scanned the choices of snacks. He thought he'd try a cheese toastie but without the salad and fries because he'd not long had his tea. He walked over to the bar to put his order in.

The jolly fat barman came along the bar towards him, wrote his order on a slip of paper, then said: 'Don't expect a culinary delight tonight mate 'cos the chef's off sick and Dot's cooking and it's definitely not what she's best at'. Then he winked at Joe and guffawed yet again, along with a couple of the blokes at the bar.

Joe was a little taken aback at the derisory comment, but his heart soared. So she was here after all. How would he be able to see her? He wasn't sure.

He sat down at his table again and waited for his toastie.

He was three-quarters through his pint when the door to the kitchen swung open and Dorothy appeared with his plate. 'Cheese toastie!' she called, looking round the bar for its owner. Joe put his hand up and a smile appeared on Dot's face, showing those pearly white teeth.

'I wasn't sure you'd come' she said, 'I got lumbered with the cooking tonight, but last orders for food are nine thirty. I could meet up with you for a drink after that, if you like?'

Joe liked the idea very much indeed. Although she was covered in an all-white overall with a cap on her head, he still found her attractive. He knew what was underneath the folds of all that material. He imagined those lovely full breasts and that luscious mountain of dark hair and found himself almost salivating just at the thought of it.

'I'll be here waiting,' he said, before adding 'looking forward to it.'

Whether she felt the same way or was just being friendly, he couldn't tell. But he would be sure when he got her in his arms and they started dancing.

She smiled and with a little wave, turned and made her way back to the kitchen.

Gradually the numbers in the pub began to dwindle and by about nine o'clock there were only six people left, all propping up the bar, drinking heavily and cracking jokes with the fat bloke. The tables were empty and nothing had come out of the kitchen for some time.

Suddenly the swing door opened and Dorothy appeared, dressed in her usual skirt and a low-cut jumper, except that tonight it was bottle green.

She went behind the bar and pulled herself a half of cider then came over and sat with Joe.

'I've just about had it here tonight, I'm all hot and bothered,' she sighed, 'how about you come to my place for a night-cap?'

'I'll have to be home by about eleven, but yes, I'd like that.' Joe replied.

She patted his hand and said 'Come on then let's go.' And to Joe's surprise, she downed her cider in one and stood up.

Her house was a tiny mid-terraced affair, a door and one window at ground level, with two above, but Joe was surprised to find it quite spacious within, due to the rooms being one behind the other.

Dot took him into the lounge, poured them both a whisky then walked over to the record player and put on a Strauss Waltz.

'OK Joe,' she teased 'let's see what you're made of.'

They took their shoes off and began dancing a slow waltz across the rug.

At first, there was an inch or two between them, but as they proceeded they became closer until eventually their bodies were pressed together. Joe felt the softness of her breasts and the thrust of her pelvis against him and for the first time in ages he felt himself hardening in his trousers. She felt it too.

'I've got a feeling that you like me,' she whispered, pushing herself against him as she said it, her mouth nuzzling his ear. 'That's the wonderful thing about ballroom dancing. Someone once said dancing was '*a desire for the horizontal expressed in the vertical.*' Whoever dreamed that up was dead right. What time did you say you had to be back?'

'Eleven. But Freda might be asleep by then, she goes up at about ten thirty usually.'

'So you could stay a little longer?' she asked, pushing ever tighter against him.

Joe was getting nervous. Things were moving faster than he anticipated.

'I would love to, but I don't think it's a good idea just yet. We don't want to put the kibosh on our meetings before we've had a chance to enjoy ourselves, do we?' Joe replied. 'I think it might be best to play it slow.'

'I don't think I can wait till next Tuesday' said Dot, 'that's a lifetime away'.

'It'll pass quickly,' he said as he gave her a peck on the cheek and broke away.

He put his shoes back on, picked up his flat cap and windcheater then grabbed her hand. 'Till we meet again, next week,' he said and he kissed it before making his way to the door.

Chapter 7

Freda and Rufus

Freda spent Saturday hunting out a pair of jeans for her next line dancing session. She had seen quite a few already in shops like *M&S* and *Dorothy Perkins* and was surprised how expensive they were.

Jeans were something that workmen wore, she'd always thought, so how could they afford those prices?

Then there was the colour. Most of the women at the class had worn faded blue ones, some with knees that looked threadbare, or had faded patches on them. She couldn't understand why anyone would buy those because they looked worn out and yet they seemed to be more expensive than the smart, freshly dyed ones.

It was not easy choosing, there were other things to consider too – hipsters or high waisted, straight legged or tapered, bootleg or bell-bottom – it was all double Dutch to her.

In the end she decided to let the decision rest with the shop assistant.

'I think Madam would look best in these,' she said, holding up a pair of straight-legged light blue hipsters. 'You could wear an untucked shirt with them to hide the bulges.'

Freda didn't think she had any bulges and took exception to the assistant's rude comment.

'I'll thank you to have a little more respect,' she said wrenching the jeans out of the girl's hands and stomping over to the changing room to try them on.

Tuesday arrived and after completing her usual schedule of tasks, Freda went up to get ready for her night out.

She thought she'd have a bath.

Standing naked in front of the mirror, she looked for the 'bulges' that the shop assistant had spotted. She turned this way and that, bent forward and backward, sat down, stood up, but was unable to find much to complain about. So she stepped into the bath for a good soak.

'Probably jealous of me being slim and her being a bit of a fatty,' she whispered to herself as she examined her toenails bobbing above the surface of the water.

She wondered whether Rufus would think she had bulges.

Once dressed and made up she went back to the mirror. The reflection didn't look much like her, she thought. The jeans didn't seem right on someone of her age and she wasn't too happy about the shirt being out either. But quite a few of the other 'gals' wore them like that too, so she wouldn't be out of place.

Freda called for Maggie at seven o'clock.

'My God!' Maggie whooped when Freda came through the front door. 'You've gone the whole hog tonight, haven't you, Freda dear, you really look the part.'

'Oh, do you think so?' Freda replied, a mixture of pride and nervousness showing on her face. She wondered what Rufus would think.

Maggie grabbed her purse and they set off for the village hall.

Rufus was already there when they arrived. He was talking to a couple of the younger 'gals', and showing them his Stetson, totally oblivious of Freda's arrival. He did have hair after all, Freda noticed, but she was a little taken aback by the friendliness he was showing to the pair.

Marlene clapped her hands and asked for people to line up. Freda rushed over, attempting to position herself next to Rufus, but the two 'gals' had other ideas about that and squeezed her out. Dejected, she wandered down the line looking for somewhere to join in.

Rufus, having disengaged from the two 'gals' was busy looking wildly around the room, as if he was expecting someone. Then his eyes fell on Freda and he visibly relaxed. He hadn't recognised her. The transformation had thrown him. He made his excuses to the two 'gals' and walked quickly over to where she was standing.

'I'd be obliged if I could squeeze in here,' he said, looking at Freda with that wonderful smile breaking across his face, 'You look great tonight Freda, I'm sorry, but I didn't recognise you with those jeans and all. You're looking absolutely fabulous.'

Freda nearly fainted with delight.

'You're looking pretty good yourself,' was the best she could muster, all of a fluster.

The woman next to Freda made space for Rufus and tried to introduce herself. Rufus acknowledged her, but immediately turned back to Freda. He seemed taller tonight she thought, well over six feet. Then she looked down at his feet. Cowboy boots! They were mid calf, tooled leather with embossed designs of galloping horses and buffalo all jumping out in brown relief from a tan background. The heels were a good two inches high.

'Wow! I love your boots,' Freda said excitedly, I'd love a pair like that.'

'I could get you a pair if you wish,' Rufus responded, 'what size are you?'

'Size 5,' she replied, 'but aren't they expensive?'

'I'll see,' was all he volunteered.

Marlene clapped her hands again and the second lesson began.

Afterwards, Rufus asked Freda to join him in a cup of tea and a biscuit before departing.

'So did you enjoy the dancing tonight?' he asked as he put a spoonful of sugar in his tea and stirred it furiously.

'I did, yes,' Freda replied, 'but I wish she'd get on to a slightly more complicated step, it's getting a little boring.'

'Agreed, but it's early days. Better to get the simple ones buttoned first then the rest might come easy. I'm thinking of getting a book of dance steps.'

'Wow! You're really into it aren't you?'

'Well, as they say, if a thing's worth doing, it's worth doing properly', and he gave her that big smile of his.

'Do you have a partner?' Freda asked, then wished she hadn't because she thought it was a bit forward of her.

'Actually no, I've reached the ripe old age of fifty-three without the help of a woman. Never really thought about marriage or anything. I know lots of women, as friends mostly, but always been too busy doing things to think about settling down with someone – till now, that is.'

'What sort of things have you been busy with?'

'Well, you know, things like travelling, I do a lot of surfing, sailing, climbing, pot-holing, all sorts really. But I'm getting to realise now that my body won't take it like it used to, so I'm easing up a bit.'

'How do you manage all that and hold down a job?'

'Don't need a job – I'm one of those lucky buggers that won the pools – got seventy five thousand on *Littlewoods* some years back and invested it to give me an income. Bought shares in *Apple* in 1980 when it went public, then *Microsoft* in 1986. I had a good financial advisor I guess. Right investments, right times, and bingo! I don't have to worry any more. I was just lucky.'

Freda just stared at him, enthralled. He was so dashing, so handsome and well off too, by the sound of it. She tried to imagine what life might have been like with someone like Rufus, then compared it with her humdrum life with Joe. She had missed out, she felt.

'Well, I'd better get home', she said resignedly, 'Joe will be wondering where I am.'

'So you're married then?'

'Oh God!' Freda thought and a lump came up in her throat. 'I've messed up.' She had never intended to mention her husband. Now she had dug a nice hole for herself. Quite against her nature, she decided in that instant, not to tell the truth. She was so afraid that it might end everything.

'It's my dog,' she said, 'he'll need a walk before bedtime.'

'OK. So why don't I come back with you and we'll walk the dog together? Where do you live?'

The hole got bigger.

'Oh God,' she thought, 'What do I say now?'

With a sickening feeling in her stomach, she turned to him and said. '18, Albert Road, but not tonight, maybe another time.'

And with that she made her excuses and left the hall.

Chapter 8

Freda and Dorothy

The following Monday morning, Freda called in at the pharmacy to pick up her prescription. She'd been suffering from some sort of rash on her neck and the doctor had prescribed some anti-histamine cream. As she waited, she saw Dorothy enter and walk over to the shelves at the back where she selected a couple of small colourful boxes. She had to pass Freda as she brought them to the till.

Freda knew Dorothy to say hello to, but they weren't what you'd call friends. She'd met her at Lucy Farnsworth's down the road, over a cup of tea one afternoon. She thought the boxes Dorothy was carrying looked like condoms.

As Dorothy passed by, Freda issued a muted 'hello Dot' and it stopped her in her tracks, hiding her intended purchase in the folds of her skirt.

'Oh, hello…Freda, isn't it? Just picking up a couple of odds and ends,' she explained, her face reddening significantly.

'Got a busy night?' Freda asked laughing.

Dot's face turned crimson. 'Got a new boyfriend,' she whispered, leaning closer to Freda, 'not taking any chances. I'll let you know how it turns out.'

'What's he like?'

'He's lovely, and he can dance, so I'll be able to get back to my passion at last.'

'Good luck with that.' Freda said.

Back at the house Freda prepared a chicken salad for lunch and called Joe in from the shed.

As they ate, she broached the story of Dorothy and the condoms that morning.

'I had to laugh,' she said. 'That Dorothy – you know, the well-built girl that lost her husband. Do you remember? The one that fell off that roof.'

'No,' said Joe, 'I don't think I ever met her.'

'Perhaps not, but today, in the pharmacy, she was buying condoms - two boxes! At her age, honestly. Said she'd got a new boyfriend who likes dancing. She must be sleeping with him or just about to. Can you believe it?'

Joe began to feel uncomfortable.

'I don't know, I don't know what she's like, I can't say I've ever clapped eyes on her.'

'You must have seen her at some point. You obviously don't remember. But anyway, as she passed by me I said 'Got a busy night?' and she went bright crimson. It was really funny.'

Joe put his knife and fork together, wiped his mouth on his napkin and said:

'Well, if there's no pudding today, I'd better get back to it now then.'

'No, there isn't till tonight.' Freda replied.

And he hurriedly disappeared back to his shed.

Chapter 9

Joe and Rufus

Wednesday morning, Joe was busy in his shed as usual when Freda came running down the path. 'The garage just rang,' she wheezed, all out of breath, 'you've forgotten to take the car for its service. They've said they can move your appointment from nine thirty to eleven o'clock.'

For almost the first time in his life, Joe swore. He checked his watch. It was ten twenty – not much time to get the car to the garage. He rushed back to the house to get his coat and keys.

At the garage, the mechanic advised that the car would be ready by around 12.30 if Joe would like to wait for it.

Joe decided to do a bit of window-shopping and call back for it.

After half an hour of walking around town, he felt tired and fancied a drink – maybe a pint of mild, he thought. The Pig and Whistle was just a few yards further up the road. He thought he'd go there for it.

The pub had only opened a short while before, but already there were a number of locals and shoppers supping at the bar.

Joe picked the last remaining barstool and ordered his pint. The chap sitting next to him turned and nodded a 'hello' and Joe nodded back. He was a big guy with bushy sideburns and vivid blue eyes.

'Probably a bit early for me, this,' said Joe, holding up his pint, 'but I'm waiting for my car to be serviced at the garage and I've got time to kill.'

'Me too,' said the big guy, 'I'm waiting for a film to be developed at the photographers. Just been hang-gliding in Derbyshire last weekend and got some fabulous pictures.'

'Wow, that sounds a bit dangerous to me,' Joe replied.

'Nothing to it, once you've taken the plunge,' the big guy replied, taking a sip of his red wine.

'I'm Joe, by the way, and you are…?'

'Rufus…Rufus Williams. Nice to meet you. Seem to be a lot of Joe's round here. Met about three over the last week – one is a dog apparently. Haven't seen it yet, but might be taking it for a walk next week.'

'Strange name for a dog.'

'Yes, belongs to a woman I go line-dancing with.'

'Really? My wife has just started doing that too, where do you go?

'The village hall where I live, near Muckleston.'

'Well, that's a co-incidence. That's where my missus goes too. You might have met her, her name's Freda, but she doesn't have a dog.'

Rufus suddenly picked up his wine and downed it in one, swivelled on his barstool and stood up.

'Sorry, Joe, I must go or I'm going to be late, nice to meet you anyway.' And he rushed out.

Joe drove the car back into his garage, closed and locked the door then went into the house. Freda was in the kitchen making a pie for supper.

'Car OK?' She asked.

'Yes, but I met with a very strange coincidence.'

'Oh yes, what was that?'

'Well, I was waiting for the car to be done and went into the Pig and Whistle for a pint. I was sitting next to a big guy who'd just done some hang-gliding in the peak district, I think it was, whose name was Rufus and does line dancing. Guess where he does it.'

'I've no idea,' Freda replied, not taking her eyes off her pastry in case they gave her away.

'Here - at the village hall. I told him you did line dancing there too, and guess what…his partner had a dog called Joe'

'My goodness, that's a strange coincidence, certainly,' Freda answered as steadily as she could, still focusing on her pastry. 'I'll have to look out for him. There's a lot of women doing the line dancing and I don't know their names yet, but I'll ask about. And I might even see them together.'

'Yes, it's funny, but until he mentioned the dog I was worried it might be you.'

Freda laughed nervously, but said nothing.

'Any chance of some lunch?' He asked.

'I'll just finish this pie, then I'll make it. Will cold ham do, with a bit of lettuce and tomato?'

'Yes, that'll be fine.'

Chapter 10

Freda and Joe

It was Tuesday morning. Joe and Freda were having breakfast – poached eggs.

'So you'll be off for lesson three tonight then?' Joe asked, as he wiped up the remnants of his egg yolk with a forkful of bread.

'Oh yes, not half,' Freda replied enthusiastically, 'I'm getting really good at it.'

Joe sat back, relieved that he would still be able to keep his date tonight with the delectable Dorothy. He'd been dreaming about her all last night.

Suddenly there was a loud knock at the door. It made Freda jump.

'Who can that be at this time of a morning?' she queried.

'Better go and see,' Joe replied.

It was the postman with a large rectangular parcel. She carried it over to the kitchen table.

'What can this be? It's addressed to me,' she said, puzzled.

'Well, hurry up and open it then and see.' Joe was getting impatient. It was not often that they got parcels – it was always exciting.

She tore open the wrapping paper and opened the box. She peeled back the tissue paper to reveal a pair of pale blue, tooled leather cowboy boots, size 5, with an envelope bearing her name. Freda was all of a tizwaz, and to make matters worse, she went scarlet with embarrassment as she read the letter:

Dear Freda,
I do hope these fit and I'm longing to see you
in them at our next meeting. Maybe you could
wear them when we walk Joe! Ha ha!
Hope you like the colour – I thought it might
suit you. Can't wait.
x Rufus.

'Oh my God!' She wailed, 'I must have an admirer.'

'Oh, so you *have* got a dog then.' Joe said, a note of sarcasm in his voice.

She looked at him straight in the eye and spat: 'What about you? Have you had it away with that Dorothy?'

'No of course not. You know I wouldn't want to upset you.' Although as he said it, he wished he had. But it'll not be long, he thought.

'So where do we go from here?' Freda asked.

'Do we need to go anywhere? We're still talking to each other and we've both got something we're keen to be involved in. Why not leave it at that?' Joe suggested.

'Are you serious?'

'Yes, why not?'

'You wouldn't mind?'

'Not if you don't.'

'What if it went too far?'

'How d'you mean?'

'Well, supposing we got...intimate, let's say.'

'Well we needn't talk about that, need we. We'd keep that bit to ourselves. Best not in this house though.

Besides, it might help us to…you know…have a bash at it ourselves.'
'Are you really serious? We haven't done that for years.'
'Yes, we could try it again, why not?'
'So we'd stay together?'
'Don't see why not. We'll just not talk about it.'

Freda got up from the table, took Joe in her arms and hugged him.
'You know, you always were such a reasonable man.' she said.

Chapter 11

Dorothy and Joe, Freda and Rufus

Christmas was fast approaching.
Freda's relationship with Rufus was blossoming although she knew she would never break away totally from Joe. Rufus too was quite happy with things. The conversation had turned to their rather awkward alliance some months previous.
'I never really wanted the wife thing,' he had said, 'I just wanted to get on with my life without having to compromise. All I was really looking for was someone to come home to, once in a while. Maybe fulfil my occasional desires, if you get my meaning. And you really fit that bill splendidly Freda.'

Freda was a renewed woman. She'd had so many new experiences with Rufus. Things she would never have considered with Joe. She'd been up at dawn walking the moors, watching the sun come up, salmon fishing on the Tweed, they'd even taken a trip to North Wales walking and climbing in Snowdonia – there was nothing she wouldn't try. Her life was exciting and it showed. She looked younger and felt healthier than at any time in her life. And suddenly, for the first time, she had a busy and extremely enjoyable sex life.

'I have to admit,' Rufus confided one day, 'I have tried this sort of a relationship before.'
'Oh, really, how long ago?' Freda was all ears.

'Yes, about ten years ago, it started out like ours, but gradually she wanted more – even wanted to marry me.'

'But you didn't want to?' Freda asked.

'No, she was married at the time, and I didn't want the hassle of breaking up a marriage, divorce and all that, so we parted company.'

'Was it amicable – the break up?'

'Well, sort of, it wasn't easy though. I felt a bit of a heel really. She seemed to think I'd been leading her toward marriage, only to drop her whenever I felt the time was right. So it wasn't exactly all sweetness and light at the final parting. But then, a couple of years later, she was widowed and she came looking for me again. That's when I realised that I didn't really want a wife. I just couldn't imagine life in an easy chair, watching TV or digging the garden. I needed more than that.'

'So you turned her down?'

'Yes, I could appreciate why she wanted to get hitched, she was a bit older than me and had been used to that kind of life, more set in her ways, if you like. She knew no different really.'

'Did you do the same sort of things with her that you do with me?'

'You mean outdoor activities?' Rufus asked, winking mischievously.

'Yes, of course I do.' Freda replied indignantly.

'Well, that was one of the problems. She wasn't keen. She liked the more gentle things like cinema, meals out, pubbing and clubbing – things like that – which reminds me, we've got to decide whether we book tickets for the Line-Dancing Christmas Party. Do you want to go?'

'Well, I think as we're still enjoying it and we now know everybody, we ought to. It'll be good fun, and it's a nice hotel.'

'OK, I'll phone Marlene and get her to keep some tickets for us.'

Joe looked at his watch – it was nine forty-five. He turned over and shook Dorothy awake.

'Come on Dot, time to get up, you'll be late for the pub.'

Dot stretched and threw back the bed covers, exposing her ample form in all its nakedness. She grabbed Joe and pulled him towards her for one last cuddle, before rising from the soft mattress and making her way to the bathroom. Joe stared after her. She was indeed a wonderful sight, he thought. Trouble was, things were getting complicated now and Joe wasn't sure what to do about it. Dot was keen to turn their affair into a union the church would recognise.

Joe had never considered the idea of divorce from Freda. He was quite happy with the arrangement as it was. Freda was a different person now and their relationship was better than ever, And of course, he had his girlfriend tucked away in her little two up two down to go to when he needed it.

Why divorce, he asked himself. What would the children think? They weren't really children any

longer, but they still might be hurt at the thought of a divorce. Besides, the current arrangement worked for both of them as far as he was concerned. He and Dot had everything they wanted didn't they?
Somehow he'd have to resolve the issue, but he didn't know how just yet.

Dorothy returned from the bathroom, having washed and donned her underwear. Joe was mesmerised, as always, by her curves carefully arranged in the slightly undersized pink lace, uplift bra and panty set. He loved taking her out to dinner or dancing – anywhere where he could show the world she was his. It did wonders for his ego – which reminded him...
'Have we decided whether we're going to the Christmas Ball with the Ballroom Dancing Club' he asked.
'Rather!' Dorothy replied. 'I wouldn't miss it for the world. We're really enjoying it aren't we? And it's a nice hotel,' she added.
'OK, I'll sort out some tickets.' Joe said.

At five o'clock, on the seventeenth of December, Joe Turnbull went upstairs to wash and change for the Ballroom Christmas party. He was calling round at Dorothy's for six.
'You're looking smart Joe,' Freda commented as he came down the stairs in his dinner suit. 'Are you off dancing again, somewhere nice?'
'Ballroom Christmas party,' he replied, donning his grey overcoat.

38

'Have a lovely time then – I don't suppose you'll be back tonight?'

'I shouldn't think so,' Joe replied, 'so don't wait up.' He pecked her on the cheek, turned and strode out of the front door.

At six o'clock, Freda went up to get ready for the line dancing Christmas party. Rufus was picking her up at seven. She had been out shopping earlier in the day and had bought a rather posh frock for the occasion. It was more than she had wanted to pay, but when she tried it on and looked at herself in the mirror she was so gob-smacked that she knew she had to have it. It looked wonderful on her and made her look so elegant – almost regal. Rufus would be so pleased, she thought.

Bang on the dot of seven o'clock, Rufus arrived, carrying a large bunch of red roses. When Freda opened the door he nearly fell over in astonishment. 'My God Freda! You look absolutely stunning. Come here and give me a hug.' Then he held out the flowers and said 'These are for you.'

Freda duly obliged, with a big kiss, then took the roses into the kitchen and stuck them in the sink with some water.

'I'll sort them out later,' she said, 'let's go or we'll be late.'

In the hotel lobby, Joe and Dorothy found a board indicating that their dinner was in the Harrington Suite at the back of the hotel next to the Fitness

Centre. As they made their way over there, they passed the main Reception Hall, gloriously decorated for Christmas with red streamers and green foliage everywhere, sprinkled generously with gold baubles and tinsel. There were chairs and tables with red tablecloths upon them, all neatly arranged around the room walls. The floor glistened in the subdued light, highly polished and ready for dancing. A band was setting up the musical equipment at the far end.

Dorothy popped her head inside the door to get a proper look.

'In for a treat tonight, no doubt about it.' She enthused, clapping her hands together and bumping Joe with her thigh.

At the Harrington Suite, most people had already arrived and were 'bagging' tables.

Table number 4 had two middle aged ladies sitting at it. Both of them were waving wildly at Joe and Dorothy.

'Over here, Joe…over here,' one of them shouted.

Dorothy waved back and they made their way over, and sat down in their allotted places, indicated by the tiny cards placed beneath their wineglasses.

The table, set for eight places, had four bottles of wine upon it, plonked in the middle next to the flower arrangement, but the two women were drinking orange juice.

'Are you two not having a proper drink? If not, it's four bottles for six of us?' Dorothy calculated. 'Looks like we'll be in for some sloppy dancing by the time we've finished in here.'

The two women laughed. That's why we're on the soft drinks. We're going to do it properly, aren't we Vera, one of them said, grabbing her partner's hand. How boring, Dorothy thought.

Rufus and Freda arrived at the hotel a little late. Poor Freda had caught her heel in a road grating which had torn it clean off. They had rushed back to the house to find another pair.

The board in the hotel lobby indicated that their suite – The Davenport, was right next to the hotel bar. And of course, that was where all the line-dancers were - in the bar, knocking back the *Budweiser* and gin and tonics. Rufus ordered a '*Bud*' for each of them and they walked over to talk to Marlene.

Freda felt the eyes of everyone in the room upon her, which thrilled her to bits. It was a feeling she had never experienced in her previous humdrum life. She was so glad she'd bought that rather expensive dress.

'You guys are on the top table - the VIP table - with me,' Marlene crooned, waiting for their grateful thanks, which didn't materialise. 'I've got a little surprise for you both.'

Freda looked at Rufus, slightly worried. She didn't like surprises. They usually turned out to be something embarrassing.

Rufus thought he'd get another round in. Marlene was halfway through a G&T and Freda, not used to drinking much, changed to a tomato juice. Rufus amended that to a Bloody Mary to loosen her up a bit, and got a whisky and soda for himself.

The Davenport Suite was quite small, but that suited the line-dancers very well, for although the group had grown in numbers, there were only 37 of them, so they needed just five round tables.

'I guess you guys haven't met our special guest? Only the greatest British country singer you Brits have ever produced…'

Marlene waved her arm toward a youngish lady with curly ginger locks surrounding a cherubic face, who was standing a few feet away talking to one of the troop.

'Over here Matilda, come an' meet my best dancers…Rufus, Freda, may I present Miss Matilda Harris.'

Of course, Freda had never heard of her – she had only just got into country music. Rufus however, was brimming with enthusiasm. He knew all her songs, all the bands she'd played with, which song got where in the charts – everything. He even got to sit next to her at the table, much to Freda's concern. However, it was alleviated somewhat when Matilda leaned across Rufus and asked: 'Hey Freda, where d'you get that gorgeous dress?' And Rufus put his arm around Freda and added 'Yes, and what's inside it is really special too.'

Things were also going swimmingly in the Harrington Suite. Dorothy was into her third glass of wine, Joe was on his second beer and talk around the table was animated. The food seemed to be late, but at least there was plenty to drink.

The faint music bouncing off the walls of the corridor and into their suite indicated that the band had started up, but it was not loud enough to impair conversation. Quite unusual that, thought Joe.

'Shall we pull the crackers?' one of the group suggested. Within seconds the idea was taken up by every table in the room and the noise of popping crackers, with their contents flying round the room, took several minutes to subside.

As Joe poured Dorothy her fourth glass, the food arrived, brought in by an army of waitresses in black skirts with white blouses, mini aprons and black stockings – turkey possibly, although it was difficult to tell, as although there was stuffing, there was Yorkshire pudding with it too. Joe thought it tasted like pork and the gravy was dark and thick enough to conceal the form and type of vegetables.

'Not the hotel's strong point, eh?' Joe ventured as they all stared at their plates.

Then there was the Christmas pudding. Dorothy wondered how they managed to give everyone a square of pudding, all the same size and thickness. She always thought Christmas puddings were round.

And she didn't think it was supposed to stick to the roof of one's mouth quite like that either. However she managed to dislodge it with a mouthful of wine then deftly poured herself another.

Chapter 12

Dorothy and Rufus

In the Davenport Suite, with the food now cleared away, The speeches began.

Firstly, Marlene stood up and called for quiet.

'Ladies and gentlemen, for those of you who haven't met her already, may I introduce our special guest tonight, Miss Matilda Harris, our finest country and western singer. She will be addressing us tonight and she has also agreed to perform her latest song in the dance hall with the band later. But before all that, I have here two little prizes one for the best 'gal' newcomer to our line dance class and one for the best 'guy'.'

Marlene looked down at the upturned face of Freda and said loudly: 'Yes, it's you Freda Turnbull, please come and receive your prize.'

Freda went bright red but was frozen to her chair.

Rufus stood up and clapped whereupon the whole room erupted calling out 'Freda!...Freda!...Freda!'

She eventually rose shyly from her chair and circled the table to where Marlene stood and was handed a small silver cup.

'Congratulations,' Marlene whispered and Freda, blushing profusely, gave a little curtsy.

'Now for the 'guy',' Marlene continued 'Yes Rufus, it's you,' and she marched round the table towards him and thrust another small cup into his hand, then reaching up, planted a kiss on his cheek. 'Well done'.

Even Rufus was a little embarrassed.
Then it was Matilda's turn to speak.

Back in the Harrington Suite Dorothy was now well oiled and thought she was ready for dancing. At least, that was until she tried to stand up. Holding the table, she walked unsteadily around it until she faced the suite entrance.
Joe rushed over to her and took her arm.
'I feel all wibbly-wobbly,' she stammered
'I think maybe we'd better go to the washroom first,' he said.
After a quick wash and brush up, Dorothy felt a little more stable, but the alcohol had made her more amorous.
'Come on Joe let's get into that dance hall and show 'em what we can do,' she mumbled, grabbing him round the waist and pushing him down the corridor, 'maybe they'll play something we can tango to.'

In the subdued light of the dance floor, Joe could see that most of their ballroom pals were already dancing. The band was playing a rock and roll number, but jiving was not his strong suit. Dorothy however, was more enthusiastic.
'Come on Joe, not your best dance, I know, but hold my hand and I'll just dance round you,' and grabbing his arm, she took off into the crowd of twirling partygoers and started jiggling away to the music.

In the Davenport Suite, Freda and Rufus were busy being congratulated by the members of their line-dancing troop. Freda was loving every minute of it. She couldn't ever remember being admired or congratulated for anything since her dad had given her away at her wedding. Certainly nothing like this had happened to her since she'd been with Joe. She was now on top of the world, brimming with confidence. She looked across at Rufus as he laughed and joked with the others – he was such a handsome, confident, self-assured being, she thought – almost god-like. And he was hers. Her chest swelled with pride and her emotions were running so high that she almost felt like crying.

Suddenly she wanted to hold him close, yet she knew that here was not the place to do it. She moved over to where he was standing surrounded by his admirers. 'Come on Rufus,' she commanded, 'I want to dance'.

In the dance hall, the band was now playing a slow waltz – just what Freda wanted. She wasn't good at dancing, but at least this one didn't require any fancy steps and she would be able to achieve her desire for closeness to Rufus. In fact the effect of the evening's alcohol intake made her perhaps a little more brazen than she should have been, but at least it was dark enough for no one to notice.

Freda's amorous moment was suddenly interrupted by a shrill voice right behind her.
'Rufus?...Rufus Williams?...Is that you?'

She turned and in the dim light, she recognised the Renoiresque Dorothy, arms around Joe's neck, a look of astonishment on her hot, shiny face.

Freda looked up at Rufus. He looked exceptionally embarrassed, she thought.

Joe had a puzzled look on his face too – he'd seen this guy before somewhere and he was racking his brains.

The dance eventually came to an end, and the hall fell silent.

'We'd all better sit down and sort this out,' Rufus said to Freda calmly, having regained his poise.

They picked a table away from the throng of dancers.

'I think firstly some introductions might be useful.' Rufus suggested.

'Oh, I don't think that will be necessary,' Joe countered, I'm sure we already know each other don't we? You, I certainly know, Rufus Williams, we met in the Pig and Whistle if you remember.'

'And I remember you Freda, from the Chemists, when I bought those condoms, if not before' Dorothy chipped in, laughing raucously, 'you know…when I had that really busy night.'

The effect of all that wine was slurring her words, to the extent that they were almost indecipherable.

'And you Rufus, how long has it been? Ten years at least, I should think.'

Freda looked confused. 'You mean…you were the one? You were with Rufus before?'

'Yep, got it in one, darling. We had a great time didn't we Rufus? Mind you, he was good looking in those days, weren't you Rufus? That's why I went for him. But you let me down, didn't you Rufus. Still, it doesn't matter any more 'cos now you're back, and I've got a new man as well and he's great. We're going to get married, aren't we Joe?'

Joe looked sheepishly at Freda.

'I don't think we've finalised that discussion yet Dot, dear. Maybe we should just change the subject and enjoy the rest of the evening. Talk about it later perhaps.' And he looked lamely at Freda again and shook his head.

'Well, there've been a lot of coincidences lately,' said Freda, 'but I think this must be the strangest of the lot. But the big question is…does it change anything?'

'It does for me, Freda dear' Dorothy said drunkenly, slapping her thigh then laughing loudly, 'I've now got my old flame back – so that's *two* people I can go dancing with, just like you and Joe. We're all going to be extremely busy by the look of it so we'll all have to book our slots. Freda, you can keep the diary.' Then, with one final raucous laugh that turned into a violent, wine-laden hiccup, she collapsed, semi-conscious, in a heap on the floor.

****

2

A Trouble Shared…

Adam, who has suffered terribly at the
hands of a relative, meets Angela, a
woman with an equally troubling
relationship. Together, they set about
resolving their problems.

Chapter 1

Confessions

It was two horrendous years since I had last called in for a drink at my local pub. At last I now felt sufficiently recovered to remedy that.

But I wondered whether I would have the courage to actually do it.

What would the locals think? I felt a little apprehensive at the thought of all those faces staring at me, asking questions or patting me on the back and saying things like 'Nice to have you back Adam', or 'Glad you're over it now'.

Yet in fact no one had come to see me in those two years. No one had offered to help. They had just carried on with their own lives. Yes, they might have discussed my plight with their partners or friends or expressed the advice they might have given me if they had bothered to see me. But no, no one had come.

It was, without doubt, the loneliest period of my life and one that I would not wish upon anyone.

But gradually I had managed to climb out of the deep rut in which I was embedded. Little by little I pulled myself up and out of the despair, sorrow, gloom and despondency that had enveloped me.

And now I had made a decision. I needed to see people - to resume communication with the world around me. So I was going to the pub – come what may.

To my surprise, there were few faces I recognised. The landlord, Fred, an overweight, jolly, red-faced chap acknowledged my presence with a 'My God! Look who it is. Welcome back Adam – good to see you again.'

And old Albert with his three teeth, bald head, holes in the knees of his dungarees and boots that hadn't been cleaned for donkey's years, gave me a wave. He always sat in the same spot – a corner by the fire, with a pint, whisky chaser and his roll-ups.

There were also two or three people I'd not met before. But that was about it.

I walked over to the end of the bar and sat on one of the three vacant bar stools and ordered a pint of the local real ale.

At the opposite end sat a reasonably attractive woman, possibly mid-thirties, seemingly arguing with an older, scruffy looking bloke in an oilskin jacket and green corduroys tucked into wellington boots. Obviously a farmer, I thought.

She didn't look happy. He was almost shouting at her and was emphasising the points he was making with his index finger, forcibly prodding her upper arm – always a sign of a nasty piece of work, I thought.

Should I go over there and calm him down? I wondered.

No, it was none of my business, but I decided that I would intervene if he got more violent.

Eventually the arm poking ceased and instead he thumped her hand which was resting on the bar with his fist, issued a loud expletive through clenched teeth and stormed out of the pub and into the street.

The woman tucked her injured hand under her armpit and sat motionless, staring into her glass. I could see she was very upset. In fact her lower eyelids glistened with tears under the down-lighters at the bar.

I felt obliged to go over to her and ask if she was all right – it was none of my business, as I said, but I was both concerned and intrigued and she looked as if she could well do with some support.

I picked up my beer and moved over to the stool that the 'farmer' had vacated.

I said 'I'm sorry to bother you, but I noticed that chap molesting you and wondered whether you need some help?'

She replied 'And you can fuck off too, I've had it up to here', her bruised hand making a chopping motion at neck level.

Then she looked up at my face and saw my shocked expression.

'Oh, my God! I'm sorry, I thought....'

'You thought I was trying to pick you up, or at best, interfering - right?' I interjected.

'Well, sort of...yes, actually.'

'No, it's just that I saw you having an argument with that farmer guy and I thought he was being a little too persuasive with his finger-poking and thumping.'

She laughed through her tears.

'He's not a farmer, he is my father-in-law, or should I say *was*. And he'd just got back from a shoot.'

That didn't really explain anything, I thought, it just intrigued me all the more.

'Your glass is almost empty, can I get you another?' I asked.

She lifted her glass and examined the remnants of her gin & tonic.

'I shouldn't really, I'm driving, but go on then, just a single…and thank you.'

I ordered another gin and a pint for myself, then tried to resume the conversation.

'Funny how people don't generally get on with their in-laws isn't it? My experience was the same.'

'I've never got on with him, right from the beginning,' she began, 'he never wanted me to marry his son. Thought I was a little too ordinary. And I had no money to change his mind. He was a bastard from day one, and now he blames me for our marriage breakdown.'

'Oh! So you're divorced?'

'No, not yet. He just found out today that I'd been to a lawyer to start divorce proceedings and thought he'd give me a piece of his mind.'

'Do you want to tell me about it?'

'Why? Are you some kind of psychologist?'

'No, nothing like that. It's just that with some people, talking about it sometimes helps. I know, because in my case no one did, and it would have.'

She hesitated for a second or two, staring straight into my eyes, her head cocked slightly sideways. She was obviously weighing me up. But then she picked up her drink and asked:

'In that case then, would you mind if we sit somewhere else, I don't really want to air my dirty washing at the bar.'

So we moved to a table in the opposite corner from old Albert, next to the blazing wood-burner in the inglenook.

She was going to open up, and if she did, then I would reciprocate, for I needed to get a few things off my chest too.

'Where to begin eh?' I offered, just to get her to start her story.

'Yes, I was just thinking that. I think I'd better start from the very beginning. I must admit that I never imagined I would end up in the sort of situation one reads about in the papers...I mean...I didn't deserve the sort of treatment I got from Rufus.'

'Rufus?' I queried, conjuring up a picture of a dog in my mind.

'Yes, my husband – stupid name really, but it suited him. He *was* a bit of a dog.'

'Talking of names', I said, 'mine's Adam...Adam Newson. I think if we are going to have a somewhat intimate conversation, we should at least introduce ourselves. Of course, I got a lot of stick at school with a name like that.'

'How d'you mean?'

'Well, it sounds like 'a damned nuisance' which was what a lot of my mates took great delight in calling me.'

'So it does!' She laughed again, 'It hadn't clicked with me. I'm Angela, maiden name Roberts but for a short while longer I suppose it will still be Hodgson.'

'Okay, Angela, nice to meet you. So, on with your story.'

'Well, this is going to sound like I'm a bit cheap, which of course I'm not, but it just happened that way. It was one of those situations that builds by itself - a bit like an epidemic.

'I was on a hen night with my friends, celebrating the forthcoming marriage of Leah, my best friend. We were being quite rowdy and had drunk a fair bit, so 'sloshed' might be a more apt description.

'In the nightclub, over by the bar, were some lads having a drink, lots of laughter and so on. We were all out of our minds and thought we'd have a bit of fun and see which of us could pick up one of those guys. Well, we all landed one. Mine was Rufus.'

'Did you like him?'

'To tell you the truth, I'd had that much to drink, I didn't care. He flashed a lot of money about that night, so I imagined he was quite well off. Anyway, he took me back to his flat and you can imagine, no doubt, where this is going?'

'I guess so.'

'Anyway, the outcome was that three or four weeks later, I was late and I found myself pregnant. I was horrified, as I had not seen Rufus since that night and dreaded having to tell him. However, after a short discussion with him over the phone, he agreed that we should get together again and if things worked out, maybe marry, if I'd have him.

'I was so surprised at his response and rather relieved at the same time, so I rather stupidly agreed. His father was vehemently against the idea and tried to talk his son out of it, but to Rufus's credit he stuck to his proposal.

We eventually ignored his father and after some time, tied the knot at a registry office. Didn't invite his mother or father, or anyone else for that matter, apart from Leah who was my maid of honour.'

'What? Not even *your* mum and dad?'

'They were no longer alive. They died in a car accident when I was thirteen, coming back from the theatre one night.'

'Oh God! That's terrible.'

She didn't comment further, but her eyes lowered to the table and there was a long pause before she took a sip of her drink and continued.

'But it wasn't long before Rufus started to show his true colours. He was the bullying type, just like his father tonight, and he could get quite nasty at times. It usually occurred after he'd lost a load of money gambling - both he and his father were gamblers.

'Anyway, I was quite scared of him. For example, if he disagreed with me over something, no matter how small, he would grab my arm and twist it, or thump me - sometimes worse. I've had my fingers bent backward till they almost snapped, been kicked on the shins, all sorts like that, just hard enough to hurt me. I won't go into what he was like in bed, but I used to hate it when he'd say 'come on' and drag me upstairs. I'd always end up with bruises somewhere. It made me realise that this was very likely the thin end of the wedge and that things would only get worse over time.

'So, for obvious reasons I didn't want it to continue. Nor did I want to bring a baby up in that sort of atmosphere. After some serious deliberation I felt that a termination would be the best solution, although I didn't have long to decide because by then I was nearly 4 months gone. To cut a long story short, I really didn't want to have anything to do with him and especially his baby, so I was hoping that this course of action would upset him to the extent that he would leave me, which he eventually did.'

'So was all this fairly recent then?'

'Yes – a few months ago and now his dad won't forgive me. He says I'd murdered his grandchild and that I'd better be prepared for some form of retribution. That's what he was reiterating in the bar tonight.'

'My God! He could be waiting outside for you.'

'Well, to tell you the truth, that's why I eventually took up your offer of a chat. It had crossed my mind that I might not reach my car safely when I left here. I wouldn't normally bare my soul like this, especially to a man I'd never met before – but I eventually felt you were a safe bet. I haven't really got any family to confide in either, you see. So I'm sorry I swore at you.'

'It's fine, don't worry, I can well understand.'

'So what about your situation. You said it was not unlike mine?'

'No, nothing like, except that I didn't get on with my in-laws either for reasons we'll come to. But before I start I need another beer. How about you?'

Angela nodded.

Walking back from the bar, drinks in hand, I had a chance to quickly appraise Angela without embarrassing her at close quarters. She was actually more attractive than I first thought – probably because by now I had more than just her looks to go on. Trim figure, voluminous, shoulder length, dark brown hair and brown eyes set in a light olive skin and a seemingly pleasant personality. Her clothes were tidy but cheap – probably supermarket quality, but overall she looked pretty nice.

God knows what she thought of me though, for I tend not to dress up much and frequently wear the same clothes I just mended the car in, even when I go out. So, I guess one can't always determine people from appearances.

'Thanks,' she said 'I shouldn't have had this drink really, but I can hardly sit here with you, empty-handed. Perhaps I should leave my car here and pick it up tomorrow.'

'Sounds a good idea to me. I can always walk you home if you don't live far.'

'Not really, it's about half a mile towards Dunston.'

'Good, that's my direction too.' I replied.

'So what about your story?'

While we'd been making small talk I had been trying to put together in my head an abbreviated but succinct version out of the horrific, mind-numbing events of the last few years of my life. But in the end I just decided to let it all come out naturally.

'OK, so it all began when I decided that I'd like to see a bit of the world. I had been working in advertising, writing articles for magazines, which were sponsored by businesses. The sort of thing headed up 'Advertisement' but under the pretext of being newsworthy, would promote someone's business. That sort of thing. In magazines like '*Woman and Home*' or '*Town and Country*', newspapers etc.'

'That sounds interesting, but could you manage to make a living out of it?'

'Yes, eventually. I had to do a lot of 'marketing' to begin with, but after my first couple of offers it really took off and I had more work than I could handle.

However, it got really boring and after a couple of years of repeating myself in print, I felt I needed to do something different. So I steeled myself into spending as little as possible and saved up my money until I reached my planned target, then I bought a ticket to the States.'

'Wow! I would have loved to do something like that but I didn't have the nerve.'

'You could have, but it'd probably be much more difficult for a single woman.' I added, 'possibly dangerous, particularly in some other countries.

'I had some distant relations living in South Carolina, near a town called Greenville - the Gibsons, although I'd never met any of them - I think my grandparents were the last of our family to contact them, but that was many years ago. The grandson was now running the place, Stanley, with his wife Julia. In their forties, so quite a bit older than me. However, I had their address so I wrote to ask if they could put me up for a few days.

'He was a scientist and something to do with forestry management. Apparently he was in great demand as a lecturer in sustainable agriculture and forestry, mainly in third world countries.

'They had inherited the beautiful, old-fashioned clapboard house originally built by their grandparents, you know the type of thing – tall columns and a portico 'porch', as they call it. Quite isolated, it looked a bit like the house *in 'Gone with the Wind'* - lots of flora and fauna around too and a quite idyllic life up to that point. He had a couple of teams of forestry workers, some being indigenous Americans. He and his wife had two young daughters about thirteen and sixteen years old and two huge golden retrievers. The sixteen-year old was very good looking and took a real shine to me. She was always following me around and asking me to take her here and there, which I was happy to do. But she was quite moody at times and there were moments when I had a feeling that she was itching to talk to me about something but it never came out.

'The mother had an upper-middle-class background and she made sure that they lived their lives as if they were in the UK. You know the sort of thing - tea and cucumber sandwiches at four o'clock - which the locals thought 'quaint'. But soon that all changed.'

'That sounds ominous. Not as a result of your arrival I hope?'

'No, not exactly, but two weeks after I arrived, we arose one morning to find that Lucy, the eldest daughter had not come down for breakfast. We wondered whether she was feeling unwell. Her mother went up to her room to check.'

'Don't tell me – she wasn't there.'

'Absolutely right, in fact the room looked a mess. Drawers pulled out, clothes all over the floor, etc. We thought there had been a bit of a struggle. We wondered whether she might have been abducted.'

'You're kidding.'

'No, we actually got the police round – typically American, four cars turned up at once – and they eventually got forensics in to go over her bedroom. It appeared that the window had been used as the escape route, either by Lucy alone, or under duress from her abductor, we didn't know initially.'

'But if she had wanted to leave by herself, there's no way she would have used the window. Wouldn't it have been too high?'

'Well, there was a lower roof, which she could have scrambled across before dropping to the ground, so it would have been possible. But at that stage we didn't know for sure.'

'But still quite a jump I would have thought.'

'That's true. But now we come to how the whole nasty business affected me. Going back a few days, shortly after my arrival, we had taken a gun and been out into the forest looking for bears – not to hunt them you understand, the gun was just for our own safety.

'Now I know that what I'm going to say sounds stupid, but it's absolutely true. I found that I didn't have any proper footwear for that sort of trekking, so afterwards Lucy took me to a mall, where I bought a suitable pair of hiking boots.

'Unfortunately, the police forensics chaps found two sets of prints in the rose-bed under Lucy's bedroom window. So they set about checking all the locals to see if any had the same pattern on their soles.'

'Oh, my God! Don't tell me that your boots had the same pattern?'

'Well, yes, but they didn't think to check that straight away. In fact when they couldn't find any boots with the same pattern on any of the locals, they went round all the places that sold boots, asking if anyone had recently bought a pair with that sole pattern. Apparently they could tell from the imprint that the boots might have been new, as the imprint showed no signs of wear. That worried me even more.'

'So did they find the guy that sold you yours?'

'Yes, and of course I was arrested.'

'But you didn't do it, did you?' Angela unconsciously moved a few inches away from me, as if she felt she might be my next victim.

'No, of course not, but the trouble was, everyone else thought I had.'

The strident sound of the bell and Fred's booming voice signalled last orders.

I didn't think I'd have time to finish my story by closing time, so I turned to Angela and quite innocently asked if she'd like to hear more of it tomorrow evening, over another drink.

She said yes, she'd love to. So I walked her home.

Chapter 2

Connections

The following evening, I decided to clean myself up a bit, have a proper shave rather than the electric one, put some decent casual clothes on etc.
I found myself thinking about Angela all night. I couldn't help liking her and although I hadn't initially set out to get involved, I found myself hoping I might find our meeting the start of a new relationship. But I had to see first what her reaction to my story would be.

Whilst walking her home, we had chatted incessantly about this and that, during which she had offered to make dinner for us both at her place before our planned second visit to the pub, but I felt that it was perhaps too premature. I tactfully suggested that it might be less hassle for her if I bought her something at the pub instead. So we agreed to meet reasonably early at the hostelry and have a sandwich with our drinks.

I arrived a quarter of an hour earlier than our planned 7 pm rendezvous. Fred automatically pulled me a pint of the real ale.
'You were deep in conversation with that woman last night, Adam.'
I knew he was hoping to find out what was going on between us.
'Has she been in here before?' I asked.

'Never set eyes on her, ever, till last night.' Fred replied.

'Strange that, because she only lives down the road.' I added.

'Tell you what', said Fred, 'if everyone who 'lived down the road' came into my pub I'd make a fortune, but unfortunately they don't, so perhaps it's not *that* strange. Never seen the bloke before either – he was being a bit of a pain. I think she was crying at one point.'

'Yes, that was her father-in-law. Not a nice guy. Her name's Angela, by the way and she's coming back here at seven for a sandwich with me.'

'Good for you,' whooped Fred, 'cracked it eh! And I could do with the extra custom.'

I winced at his remark, after all, I had not really set out to 'conquer' her.

'Make it a special one – the sandwich.' I said.

At precisely 7 pm Angela turned up, all dolled up but looking dejected. Her face brightened somewhat when she saw me sat at the bar.

'Hi,' I said, 'is everything OK? You don't look very happy.'

'No, I'm not really, I couldn't sleep last night. Not after I'd had a late visitor,' she replied, 'my damned father-in- law again.'

I saw Fred cock an ear and start sidling towards us.

'Let's go and sit by the fire.' I suggested.

I chose the old pew with the red cushions and we sat side by side at the table out of the direct heat of the wood-burner.

'You can tell me about it. What did he want?'

'God! It was terrible – he turned up at about ten minutes after midnight, and when I tried to shut the door on him he forced his way in, grabbed me by both arms and threw me onto the settee. I wasn't sure what he was going to do, but I was very scared. He pinned me down, leaned over me and snarled that he wanted money – more than I've got.'

'What on earth for?'

'He said that if I wanted him off my back, it would cost me five thousand. He said if I didn't have it by Friday, something terrible would happen, but he wouldn't say what that might be.'

'Surely he was just bluffing,' I ventured, although I wouldn't have been keen to test my theory. 'What on earth can he have on you that would be worth five grand?'

'Because there's something else – something I felt I couldn't tell you yesterday...' Angela hesitated and her eyes welled up with tears.

'I held something back. Stupid of me really...but I wasn't really sure about you then...Rufus is dead.'

'Christ!...But hang on, I thought you said you were getting a divorce?'

'Yes, I did, I'm sorry, but I wasn't sure whether I should have been telling you the proper story – I hadn't even had a chance to really get to know you – so I edited it a bit.

'But last night, after you dropped me off, I thought about it a lot and after hearing your problems and of course, your readiness to tell me about them, I thought I should reciprocate and come clean with mine.'

'I suppose I can understand your logic. But is that the only thing you didn't want to tell me?'

I shouldn't really have said that, I thought, as I noticed the hurt look on her face.

'Of course,' she replied, indignantly, 'I'm telling you everything now.'

'Yes, sorry, I didn't actually mean it to come out quite so abruptly as that...sounded a bit as if I was interrogating you, which of course, I'm not. Let's get back to Rufus – what happened to him?'

'I really don't know – he went off in his car with a rubber hose and a bottle of whiskey. My immediate thought was that he was just so upset that I'd taken matters into my own hands and decided to get rid of the baby. I had no idea that he was the type to let something like that make him commit suicide.

'A walker found the car in the woods with him in it, the rubber hose in through a window from the exhaust pipe and the whiskey bottle was empty. The engine was still running apparently, so the police were able to roughly guess the time of death. It was more or less after we'd had our final row about the termination, when he left me.'

Angela was now quietly crying.

'For God's sake Angela, there must be more to it than that. I know I didn't know the bloke, but from what you've said about his nature, it didn't sound like he was the type to commit suicide just because his wife had a termination without telling him.'

I was trying to make her feel less responsible for his action.

'For a start, he may have been threatened over a debt or something, like his father, or maybe he and his father didn't get on any more. Furthermore, you don't know what else he was up to, or whom he was involved with. There could have been any number of reasons.'

'I know I hated him, but I never wished him dead. But I do wonder whether my action was the last straw as far as he was concerned' Angela replied.

'You mean the termination?'

'Yes.'

'But you had every right and plenty of reasons to do what you did. He was a nasty piece of work, he was an abuser and you feared that he would get worse. Just imagine what sort of father he would have been.'

'Tell that to my father-in-law, he's lost his son and his grandson. He's going to come after me if I don't pay him off and I can't.'

Angela started crying quietly again.

All of a sudden I felt slightly sick. It occurred to me, fleetingly, that all this might be a scam. Was she expecting me to say that I would raise the five thousand for her, after which she would waltz off with the money and the 'father-in-law' and find some other gullible sod? Was he *actually* her father-in-law? Was all the finger-prodding at the bar designed to get a punter interested and ensnared?

No, surely not. Looking at Angela now, she seemed too nice for that, and besides, she really did appear totally distraught.

However, I was not totally prepared for her next move.

'If I can't get the money by Friday I can't go back to my place because he'll come looking for me. Can I ask a big favour of you?'

I guessed what was coming and I realised that I was going to get drawn into this terrible saga of hers. As if I needed any further aggro – I had my own problems to contend with. But she looked so forlorn and I was weakening minute by minute. I was by now developing feelings for her.

'I think it might be a good idea if you stayed at my place on Friday - for a few days - just until it all blows over,' I heard myself saying.

She looked up at me through her tears and took my hand and squeezed it.

'Oh thank you, thank you so very much, that's what I was trying to pluck up the courage to ask you.'

'But on no account do you pay this guy any money,' I said sternly, 'it would not be the last time he threatens you.'

'No, of course not. I couldn't anyway.'

'OK so how about I buy us both a drink and we get that sandwich?'

She smiled, albeit weakly, for the first time that evening.

I ordered the same drinks as we'd imbibed the night before and asked Fred to organise a couple of avocado and bacon baguettes, the house speciality sandwich.

Back at the table, we continued our conversation.

'I'm so sorry,' Angela said, 'we were supposed to be continuing your story tonight, shall we move onto that?'

'OK,' I replied but before we do, and having just given your dilemma second thoughts at the bar, I think it might be better if you moved in with me tonight. Your father-in-law might just change his mind over the Friday deadline and conjure up something new in the meantime. Maybe pay you another visit, God forbid. We can collect your stuff in the morning. You can borrow some of my wife's nightwear.'

'I guessed you might have a wife,' Angela said, 'You mentioned having in-laws. I wondered where she fitted in.'

'*Had* a wife' I said, 'she's no longer with us I'm afraid.'

'Oh my God! You poor thing – and there was I being selfish and piling all my troubles onto you.'

She touched my arm.

'What happened?'

'I think it's probably best if I continue my story,' I said, 'and we'll come to that later.'

I didn't want to go over it all again at this point. Nor did I want us both to be crying.

At that moment, Fred's equally overweight daughter appeared with the food and asked if we'd like any condiments.

Fred had done us proud. We had French fries and salad with the baguettes, which was not the norm.

'Just a little salt for the fries,' I suggested. She waddled off to get it from the bar.

'So where did I get to? Oh yes, I'd just been arrested. All the police had was a boot imprint that matched mine and a shop worker who remembered me buying them and identified me in a line-up at the station.

'At that point no one had even considered whether the boot print and my boot were the same size. I was hoping that this might be the one aspect that would save me, but as luck would eventually have it, the sizes *were* the same.'

'What size were you?' Angela asked.

'UK size 8, I forget the American equivalent – 8.5 I think it was.'

'But that's a most common men's shoe size. They can't hang a case on that, surely? '

'No, but it persuaded a lot of people, including the Gibson family.'

'So what happened next?' Angela was getting impatient.

'They kept asking me what I'd done with Lucy – why did I abduct her – had I raped her – was she still alive – all sorts of horrible things.

'Then there were the newspapers. Apparently some little squirt in the police had talked to the press and convinced them that I was the abductor and that because Lucy was not found she must be dead and hidden somewhere.

'That set off every red-neck Tom, Dick and Harry in the neighbourhood searching for her. They came in droves, with picks and shovels in the back of their battered King-cabs, all assuming that I'd buried her somewhere.

'I had Lucy's father, Stan coming to my cell and pleading with me to come clean, but as I was not involved I couldn't say anything. The police rather nastily relayed this to the press as me exercising my right to remain silent, which as far as everyone was concerned, just added another layer of proven guilt.

'I realised at this stage that I needed a lawyer, but I knew they would not come cheap and I wondered whether I would have sufficient funds. However, the police gave me a list of local lawyers, so I threw caution to the wind and picked one out.

'Luckily for me, I happened by chance to have picked a good one, for at the trial, as long-winded as it was, the case was thrown out for lack of evidence. But Lucy was never found.

'I got thrown out of the house by the relatives and I was given so-called 'police protection' (which turned out to be virtually non-existent) until the first available flight back to the UK, by which time I was just about cleaned out.

'Though I had no money, I was so glad that I had taken the decision not to sell my flat as I was able to virtually pick up my old life where I left off.'

Angela was so engrossed in my story that she had not even taken a bite of her food, so we broke off to eat. However, she couldn't contain herself for long.

'So where did your wife fit in to all this?' She asked between mouthfuls.

'Well she hadn't arrived on the scene at that point. I didn't meet her for another couple of months or so. I first set eyes on her at a drinks party held by one of the magazines I was writing for. She was working for the National Archives at the time. We hit it off and about six months later got married. I sold my flat and we bought a house together – the one you'll be staying in tonight.'

'Do you want to talk about what happened to her?'

'Do you really want to hear?'

'Well…yes, If you don't mind. I'd like to get the full picture. We can both be totally candid can't we?'

'Of course, I think I can tell you, I'm just about over it now, although I have my off days and I'm still sore about the injustice of it all.'

She put her hand on my arm again, reassuringly. 'If it hurts, leave it for now,' she said.

I felt the warmth from her hand and saw the look in her eyes – she was totally sincere. How could I ever have misjudged her motives.

'No, I can tell you. We'd been married for just seven months, we were sitting up in bed one evening, discussing our future, babies and things like that, when there was a familiar squeaking noise on the landing – a floor board deforming. There was someone in the house.

I quietly got up, motioned to Jenny – that was her name – to keep silent and I went to see who or what it was, but I didn't put the light on as I thought it would have alerted the intruder. Unfortunately that was a mistake, for the door burst open and a torch beam passed around the room and over the bed, then two shots were fired. One hit me in the leg and the other fatally wounded my wife.'

I found myself telling this part of my story in a very matter of fact way, largely because I felt I might otherwise break down. I just hoped that Angela wouldn't see it as me being uncaring. But when I looked at her she was weeping.

'I can't believe this, you poor man, who on earth would have done this to you, especially after everything you'd already been through.'

'Well, I didn't find out for a while. The intruder fled across the landing with me crawling after him and he shot down the half flight of stairs where there was an open window. He'd obviously come in through there. He jumped out.

'I crawled back to the bedroom, to find Jenny unconscious but still breathing awkwardly. She had been shot in the chest. I called an ambulance and the police, but Jenny died in my arms before they arrived.'

That was the point at which I broke down. Angela put an arm around me.
'You poor, poor thing, please don't go on. I hate seeing you so distressed – it must have been absolutely awful for you.'

But I eventually found the strength to continue. This was the first time I had spoken to anyone about it and I realised that I had to do it, even though it involved reliving the event. I had to get it off my chest as it were, and now that I had said it I knew that the most harrowing part of the whole story was over.

'The police found the intruder very quickly – he had skewered himself through his lower abdomen on the beanpoles below the window. Apparently he was bleeding heavily and was crawling away on his hands and knees.

The ambulance arrived and both Jenny and I were whisked off to the local hospital.

I was totally numb and confused but felt detached at the same time. It hadn't yet fully sunk in – it was like a bad dream. I couldn't understand why it had happened. What was the motive? Who had done this? And of course, I had lost the love of my life.'

'So how badly were you injured?'

'I had been shot in the leg and the bullet had shattered my femur about halfway up. But it was apparently a reasonably simple fix, the surgeon said, by pinning the two bits together, and before too long I was walking on it again.

But while I was in hospital I had a visit from the police. They wanted to know if I knew a guy called Stanley Gibson, but they didn't say why.

Well, of course I did. It was Lucy's father. I immediately knew why they asked, but I couldn't believe it. Had he killed Jenny?'

'I'm afraid so,' the policeman had replied, 'he has actually confessed. He still had the gun on him when we apprehended him and we've got a match with the slug from your leg. His blood matched that found on the runner beans in your garden, so he could hardly deny it.'

'Apparently he was over in the UK for a talk to a group at Bristol University, but by my reckoning he probably engineered the trip as an alibi to cover the shooting.
He clearly believed that I was Lucy's killer and wanted the justice that the courts wouldn't give him.'
'But you were a relation of his,' Angela chipped in, 'wouldn't that cast doubts in his mind?'
'Well, you have to remember that until I got there we didn't really know each other – we only knew *of* each other. So we could just as easily have been total strangers with totally different traits and behaviour. We probably only shared about half a percentage point of DNA. I think he was about my third or fourth cousin.'

'Wow! So if he felt so strongly about you having been the perpetrator, what about all the others back in Greenville. Will someone else take up the reprisal?'
'No, I can definitely confirm that there will be no further vengeance.'
'How can you be so sure?'

Fred's rotund little daughter returned and interrupted our conversation by asking 'Is everything alright'. They seem to do that nowadays in most eating establishments. I always feel like saying 'Yes, everything's fine but the food's pretty terrible, now leave us alone.' But of course, I didn't.

I was getting to the part of my story that hurt me almost as much as Jenny's demise and which largely contributed to the cause of my two years of total despair and solitude, but I couldn't tell Angela yet.

'I need to resume this story at my place,' I began, 'There is something there that I want to show you. Then you will fully understand why I know there will be no further action and you too will experience the enormity of the injustice that sent me into a spiralling decline from which I thought I would never recover.'

'But you will tell me tonight, won't you?'
'Yes, of course, but in the meantime let's see if we can resolve your own predicament.'

I had only known this woman for a day or so, yet already I felt as if I'd known her for years. Here I was, telling her intimate details of my life as if she were a close relative. And she was doing the same, to me. There was clearly mutual trust and of course, I was warming to her at a phenomenal rate.

'So, how do we get this father-in-law of yours off your back? What do you know about him? Any dirt?' I asked.
'Well, I suppose that he must have debts, because he's demanding money, which is unusual in the circumstances. I could better understand it if he

wanted to beat me up or run me over in his car or something, but to ask for money seems somehow disconnected from any normal reaction one would expect in that situation.'

'Quite agree. So maybe resisting any payment might make matters worse for him. If he owes that much and can't pay it himself, then he's hardly likely to get the money any other way other than from an equally nasty loan shark. So we keep the pressure on.'

'I notice that you said 'we'. Does that mean you are going to help me rid myself of this problem?'

'Well, I think after all we've told each other, it's only right that we should jointly try to resolve our problems.'

Again her hand came out and grabbed my arm, but this time she pulled it towards her, forcing me to lean over and allowing her to reach up and give me a peck on the cheek.

'Oh you wonderful man, you really cannot imagine how relieved I am that I have met you. I feel so much better about all this. You were right. Talking about it to someone caring is such a tonic.'

'The feeling is mutual, to be sure.' I replied.

Perhaps that sounded a little tamer than the way I felt inside, for I was now convincing myself that this woman was going to accompany me into my future.

'OK so we don't pay – but how do we stop him taking reprisals?'

'We go to the police and make a complaint. You can start with 'assault' and then add 'demanding money with menaces', both of which are reasons to press charges.'

'But then, even if he goes to jail, he'll be let out later and still hunt me down.'

'Only if he can find you.'

'But we need something else, something more.'

'OK. What about his wife – does she exist?'

'Yes, but I've tried to keep her out of it because she's actually been quite nice to me. She's a very submissive type and unfortunately will go along with anything her husband does or says just to keep the peace.'

'Does she love him...I mean do they still have a normal relationship? Or does he beat her up too?'

'No and yes he did beat her up sometimes, but she would deny it, as I say, just to keep the peace.'

'What about Rufus. Did he have money? You said he was splashing it about a bit when you met him.'

'I don't think he could have done because I haven't got anything from him and I was his wife. We had a joint bank account, which was up and down like a yo-yo, mainly down, but whether he had any money elsewhere I have no idea. I'll have to wait until it's all finalised with the solicitor.'

'Well the longer we wait for that, the less chance your father-in-law has of getting any money out of it too, so that's all to the good. But how are you surviving now?'

'With some difficulty, I can tell you. I think I'm going to have to sell the house. There's no way I can keep up the mortgage payments. I got a big payment put into a trust when my parents died, but unfortunately, between paying the deposit on the house, furnishing it and bailing out Rufus from time to time from his gambling debts, there's little left to help me now.'

'Right, so we sleep on it and try and come up with something tomorrow. Let's have another drink.'

'Why don't we have one at your place – seeing as I'm staying the night? Shall I buy a bottle to take back with us?'

'No need. There's a couple at home.'

So I paid the bill and we left the pub and walked, arm in arm, back to my place.

Chapter 3

Resolutions

I liked the close proximity we shared on the way home and I could tell that she was happy with it too. I could see that we were going to get on and that if I played my cards right we would become 'an item' as they say nowadays. But strangely enough it wasn't a sexual thing. On further analysis, I think it developed largely from the fact that we had both been so depressed, isolated, and lonely, overburdened with our problems, with no support, that we desperately clutched at the friendship that was developing between us. As they say: 'A trouble shared is a trouble halved'. There was no doubt in my mind that we were growing fond of each other too.

'So would you prefer red or white?' I asked as we settled on the stools in the kitchen.
'Red for me, I think, unless you've got a bottle opened, in which case either.'
'Red it is then.'
I poured two glasses and opened a packet of nibbles and chucked them into a bowl.
Raising my glass, I said 'Welcome to my humble abode and let's hope we can sort out our troubles together.'
We clinked glasses and she responded with 'Thank you for putting me up and being so understanding and kind.'
We paused conversation for a few minutes as we sipped our wine and sampled the nibbles. We just

sipped and smiled at each other. The electricity between us was palpable.

I broke the silence.

'OK, so let's get back to your problem. In a way, the plan I had decided upon for resolution of my own problem may also help to resolve yours, but only if we can mutually agree to it.'

'Intriguing. What did you have in mind?'

'Well, I can no longer stay in this house, not with the constant reminder of Jenny everywhere in here. Whilst I don't ever want to forget her, I don't wish to dwell on what might have been either.'

'No, I can understand that, but I don't see the connection.'

'Of course not – not yet, but, as you said yourself at one point, you'd like to travel...Look, I'm finding this quite difficult to put into words, and I hope you won't be offended if I say it, but I'm going to anyway...I'm actually falling for you.'

'Oh, my goodness! Are you going to propose or something?'

'Would you be upset if I did?'

'On the contrary, I would be flattered, but I would probably suggest that we get to know each other a little better before we make up our minds.'

'So that wouldn't be a 'No' then?'

'Well, I don't see you as a damned nuisance, Adam Newson, in fact I'm rather taken by you. But how will it resolve my situation?'

'Well, as you have said, and as I had mentioned before, I too have always had this urge to travel. And, coupled with my desire to sell this house and you yours, I thought that the resolution to your problem would be for you to travel with me, hopefully perhaps one day, as my wife.'

'I would love to travel and I would be delighted for us to do it together, so come here you big softy and give me a hug.'
She slipped off her stool and rushed over to mine and we embraced. She felt warm and supple and it felt good. For the first time in ages, I felt human again.

After some minutes, she pulled away. 'But you haven't told me the rest of your story. You were going to explain why you ended up in that spiralling decline, remember?'
'Oh yes,' I said. 'Hang on a minute, I'll just get what I wanted to show you.'

I went over to the sideboard by the dining table and sifting through the papers in the drawer, took out a letter and handed it to her.
'Read that, but put yourself in my place, with all that has gone on, and tell me how you would feel. You can read it out loud.'
Angela opened the airmail letter and started reading:

'Hi there Adam,

Just thought I would drop you a line to say how sorry I am to have caused you so much heartache with the cops over here. I never meant to upset you.

I just had to get away from Dad. My friend Dan agreed to take me away after the last, really horrid episode – he's an Indian from the Narragansett tribe. Dad's an absolute perve. I just couldn't tolerate it any longer.

Dan took me up to the Indian Reservation in the Smoky Mountains to hide away. I'm going to write a note for Mum to say I'm OK, Dan will drop it in the mailbox at the house, but I can't tell anyone where I am because I know Dad will come after me and probably bring half the village as well. Dan will probably be sacked or, worse still, be beaten up and maimed for life and I will be brought back home for him to continue his awful abuse. I'm just fearful that that will be the eventual outcome.

Anyway, sorry again for making life so difficult for you and I'm sorry I have no way of remedying the situation. Glad though that you got off at the trial. Hope you got back to the UK OK.
Keep mum about me. All the best,
Lucy'

'Oh my God! I can't believe it. That's awful. After everything you went through, and losing your wife too. Of course, she won't have known about that – it probably never got into the American papers. But surely she must know that her father is now in jail?'

'Not necessarily, it sounds as if she is still out of contact with the family. Hence the 'Keep mum...' in the letter. Besides, it might have taken a while for the letter to reach me, so she may not have heard of his arrest when she wrote it.

'But what got me the most was all the hurt that was caused by the behaviour of one terrible man. I can't blame Lucy for her actions, as she probably had no one to confide in. I doubt her mother would have believed her either, if she had broached the subject. Do you remember that I said I thought she had something on her mind, which she was itching to talk about? That must have been it, obviously. She'd have had no idea of the repercussions that were to ensue. But for me to get dragged into it and for it to spill over into my home life here in UK, losing Jenny and everything, well, it just sent me right down to rock bottom.

And all because I wanted to do something different with my life.

Well I certainly did that.'

'Yes but you can't blame yourself either – you didn't know Jenny then and it was just a case of following the route destiny took you.

'Now look at how your misfortunes have affected me. Suddenly my life is full of positives. Your troubles have led you to me, helped me to resolve mine. I've come out of the doldrums, found a lovely man to help me do it and now I look forward to a long and happy life hopefully with him, travelling the world, both of us free of our encumbrances, free as the birds of the air. Nothing can replace what you have lost, but if I can help fill the void in your life, and you mine, then we will *both* be able to look forward to a life fulfilled.'

And she approached me again and threw her arms around me.

'Can I take that as a yes then?' I asked.
'Do I *have* to have the spare room tonight?' She countered.

****

3

Growing Pains

The fortunes, misfortunes, misery and elation experienced by Tommy, a young boy growing up in the second half of the 20th Century

1951

First Love

So, what do you think of it Tommy?' His dad asked as Tommy tried out the tricycle, skidding across the toyshop floor.

'It's smashing, Dad, can I have it?'

'Well you'll have to accept that it will be your 5th birthday present *and* next Christmas' present, Tommy, 'cos we don't have money to burn. As it is, you're only getting it 'cos your mum saved up all her pennies and ha'pennies for a couple of years. I just found them in a jar under the stairs. If she could see you now on that tricycle I believe she'd be right proud of herself, and so she should be, I can tell you.'

Tommy thought about his mum. He imagined her standing there in the shop, looking down at him on the tricycle, smiling at him. He missed her so much. She had been his mainstay – the one he ran to when he needed help or when he grazed his knees, or even just when he needed the answer to some taxing little problem he was having difficulty sorting out. She never fobbed him off or told him she was too busy. She was always there to help him, console him, cuddle him and make him feel warm and safe. Tommy was her life. But now she was gone.

Tommy didn't understand what had happened to her. His dad just said that she had 'got ill'. She was taken to the hospital and never came back. His dad wouldn't take him to see her – he said she'd changed so much he wouldn't like it. Tommy cried for days.

As he sat there on his new tricycle he offered up a little prayer to his mum and then, out loud, he finished it with a 'thank you'.

His dad searched in his pocket and pulled out a length of twine. 'If you want, you can ride it to the bus stop Tommy, but I'll have to keep a hold on you with this bit o' string tied to the seat.'

'That'll be nineteen shillings please,' said the shopkeeper, holding out his hand. Tommy's dad reached again into the pocket of his coat and with some difficulty pulled out the jam jar packed with coppers.

'I think you'll find that's correct,' he said.

The shopkeeper tipped the coins out onto the counter and counted it out twice before putting two coins back in the jar and returning it to Tommy's dad. The rest he poured through cupped hands into the cash register and issued a receipt whereupon Tommy and his dad left the shop.

Tommy had never ridden a tricycle before, but he found it no trouble – in fact his dad had to break into a trot to keep up with him.

Tommy thought about his mum as he pedalled. 'She'll be looking down at me, really proud of how quick I learnt to ride it,' he said to himself.

Back at home, he rode around the back yard several times until he was called in for tea. He parked the tricycle in the yard by the lavvy, where he could admire it through the window as he was eating. It was the best thing his mum had ever bought him.

1952

First friend

Tommy heard the whinny of a horse in the road outside the house. He looked out of his bedroom window and saw a big shire pulling a cart loaded with furniture and cases. It stopped at the house next door and a man and woman stepped wearily down to the pavement, swiftly followed by a boy of about his own age.

'Dad...Dad...there's a cart outside with chairs and tables an' things on it.'

'Aye lad, most likely it's the new people movin' in next door. They'll get a shock when they get in, I'll bet. The place has been empty for years.'

'And there's a boy with 'em too,' Tommy said excitedly.

'Well, before you get *too* excited and want to go round to play, we'll have to see what type of folk they are, lad. I don't want you mixing with the likes of tinkers and their sort.'

'What are they, Dad?' asked Tommy

'Never you mind, lad, just hope that they aren't, that's all.'

It wasn't an answer. In fact all it did was made Tommy more curious. He went out into the yard and peered through the fence to see if he could determine what type of people they were.

While the parents were unloading the cart and carrying stuff into the house, the boy was playing with a bucket and a stick, adding some mud, which he was digging from the old vegetable patch with a rusty trowel.

Tommy was fascinated.

'What's that you're doin'?' He called through the fence.

The boy jumped at the sound of Tommy's shrill voice. He hadn't seen him there.

'I'm makin' worm sloppy,' he replied.

Tommy was none the wiser.

'What d'you do with it?'

'Nothin' much,' the boy replied, 'what's yer name?'

'Tommy, what's yours?'

'Darren,' the boy replied.

'What does your dad do for a job?' Tommy asked.

'He's a teacher. We've moved here 'cos he's goin' to teach at the village school an' I'll be goin' there too.'

Tommy sighed with relief and without further ado, rushed into the house to tell his dad and get his approval to play with his new friend, Darren.

Tommy's dad folded the newspaper, got up from his chair by the stove, knocked out his pipe on the hearth and looked down at Tommy with a flicker of a smile on his face. 'Well, I suppose we'd better introduce ourselves,' he said quietly, 'let's pop round there now an' see if they need any help.'

The pair walked down the path to the gate and were just in time to see the man and woman struggling to get an upright piano down off the wagon.

'Hold on there missus, shouted Tommy's dad, 'I'll give yer a hand wi' that.' And he rushed over to take the weight off the woman's arms.

The man was on the wagon, pushing the piano off the back. The weight of the free end was beyond the ability of the helpers to support it as it careened over the edge of the tailgate, and it dropped to the ground with a thump and a strident twang as the strings hummed with the shock of the fall.

'Most likely youd've had to re-tune it anyway,' volunteered Tommy's dad, 'the names Archie, …Archie Norton an' this is my lad, Tommy.'

'I'm John…John Blake and this is my wife Mary,' said the man, eyeing up the damage to the end of the piano, 'and this is our boy Darren. I never want to go through moving ever again, it's a real nuisance.' He added.

'Have yer bought the place then?' Archie enquired.

'No we're just renting till we can get a deposit together to buy a place of our own in a couple of years,' replied John.

'Looks like just the beginnin' of yer troubles,' Tommy's dad suggested, 'the house an' garden are goin' to take some sortin' as no one's lived here for years. Tell yer what, let's get the rest o' yer stuff off the wagon an' y'can come round to ours for a cuppa tea. What do y'say?'

The suggestion was taken up with enthusiasm and all six of them fell into the task of emptying the wagon as fast as possible.

'I can take the horse and cart back to the undertakers later,' John said, 'they need it for tomorrow.'

As they sat round the stove supping their tea, John resurrected the conversation about the state of their new home.

'I don't suppose I'll get time to do the house *and* the garden if I'm teaching at the school, we may have to look for a gardener.'

Mary nodded.

Tommy's dad sat up, slowly reached over to the table, put down his mug and rubbed his chin.

'Don't see many gardeners in these parts John, I'm here all day workin' on me vegetables an' I can spare a bit o'time, so mebbe you'd be best lettin' me do it for yer. How does a two shillin' an hour sound to yer?'

'Sounds quite reasonable,' John beamed, 'but I couldn't afford more than one day a week.'

'Lets say 2 hours a day for weekdays,' Tommy's dad offered.

The deal was done and Tommy's dad sat back in his chair with a broad grin on his craggy face. He had needed a few extra bob in order to keep his dwindling finances afloat.

1953

Disappointment

It was almost May and Tommy's dad was making good progress in tidying up the Blake's garden. He'd managed to remove the masses of brambles that had virtually taken over the plot during the years of neglect. He'd dug out a couple of ash trees that had sprung from nowhere and levelled and re-seeded the lawn.

Every morning at ten o'clock Mary would bring him a mug of tea as he toiled, and slowly they began to develop a close friendship.

Archie became quite enamoured with Mary and it wasn't long before he was suggesting that he extended his gardening hours.

'Don't worry about the extra money, Mary, I'm doin' it 'cos I'm enjoyin' it,' he would say each time she offered him an additional florin out of her housekeeping money.

Then she stopped bringing him tea outside and instead suggested that he might like to come in, wash his hands and sit down and have a bit of cake with it.

By June Archie was seldom at home. He'd be round at Mary's making suggestions about new plants for the garden or which fruit trees would be the best for producing bumper crops.

'I'd be happy to put 'em in for you, Mary,' he'd say.

And of course, Mary was flattered, even entranced by his attention.

Then it was July and the schoolchildren broke up for the summer.

John was home most of the day, and Archie's dalliance had to stop. Or at least he'd have to pick his time.

It was September 21st when everything went wrong for Tommy. He too had struck up a close friendship with Darren, but that day, just one week into the new term, he got home to find the house next door empty again.

'What's up with next door, dad? There's no one there no more.' Tommy asked, worried.

Archie reddened with embarrassment. 'Search me Tommy, they all of a sudden upped sticks and took all their stuff with 'em. Mebbe he got the sack from the school or summat.' He struck a match on the side of his corduroy trousers and carefully applied the flame to his pipe, intermittently sucking and puffing until it was evenly lit. He was giving himself time to think before expanding on his hastily invented theory as to why the Blake's had left in such a hurry.

'It's a damn nuisance too 'cos you know what that means, don't yer, Tommy. We've lost me two shillin' an hour, for the gardening, so we're goin' to have to tighten our belts again.'

'But Darren was at school today, an' he said nowt about it Dad, I just don't get it. He would've told me 'cos I'm his mate.'

'Sometimes things happen like that son, I guess we'll never know,' his dad replied.

Tommy went up to his room and laid on his bed, upset. It just didn't make sense. Then he had an idea. If Darren *was* still at school tomorrow, he'd ask *him* what it was all about. Maybe a house had come up and his Dad was ready to buy it? Perhaps it was that simple. If that was so, then Darren would definitely be at school tomorrow and they'd still be friends. He'd be able to invite him over to his house occasionally, maybe even stay the night sometimes. Maybe he was worrying over nothing after all.

He'd have to see.

But it was not like that. Yes, Darren was at school, but he didn't want to talk to Tommy.

'My dad says I'm not to play with you no more, Tommy.'

'What d'you mean?'

'I've not got to see you no more.'

'Why? What's happened? Tell me Darren.'

'I dunno, do I? But summat's happened.'

'Yer dad hasn't bought a house then?'

'No, we've moved to another place in Burgess Hill, so I won't be able to play with you no more anyway.'

Tommy was distraught. He'd lost his first real mate, and yet he knew not why.

1955

Awareness

It was Sunday, a very hot afternoon, perhaps the hottest Tommy could remember in his short life. As they sauntered along the lane, he took his penknife from his pocket and began whittling away at the branch of elder he had torn from the hedge. His friend, catapult in hand, was firing small stones into the air and watching them drop onto the lane ahead of them. Mick, an older pupil from the school, had become Tommy's friend when Darren moved to Burgess Hill, largely because no one of Mick's own age seemed to get on with him and he lived close by.

The tinny sound of a bell rang out behind them and the two boys moved to the side of the unmade road as the vicar approached on his ramshackle bicycle, swerving from side to side to avoid the meadow-sweet tumbling over the bank into the road, his cassock flailing around his legs.

'Up to no good again I see,' he called out to them jovially, as he passed by, his legs pumping away on the pedals, perspiration shining on his receding forehead.

'I had hoped to see you in church today. Do make sure you're there next Sunday,' he wheezed as he disappeared round the corner.

'Fuck that!' said Mick.

His expletive reminded Tommy to enquire as to Mick's previous evening's endeavour.

'Did you do it last night, like you said? Tommy enquired of his friend as he whacked down the meadow sweet at the side of the road with his elder wand.

'Nah!' Mick replied with disdain. 'She's a right little teaser that Marion, 'cos after all the playing around, just as I thought we were gonna do it, she upped an' ran off.'

'But did she do what you said she would? You know…' Tommy gesticulated to illustrate his query.

'Yeah! We did a bit of that but she stopped after a while, saying that I stank of summat.'

'What was it like?'

'What?'

'You know…what you said she'd do.'

'Yeah! It would've been great if she'd carried on, but she never. She just ran off.'

Mick, in his frustration, kicked the loose gravel with his scuffed boot, the small stones bounding down the lane in all directions. 'Shan't bother with her no more, I'll see her in school, but I'm never going out with her again, she's had her chance.'

Tommy slowed to a standstill and looked at Mick. 'Do you think she'd do it with me?' He asked.

'I don't think she'd want people to know that she'd done it with a boy three years younger than her, so I s'pose the answer is 'No', if you want the truth.'

Tommy didn't want the truth. He had always wanted to be with Marion, from the first day he set eyes upon her. He loved her face, surrounded by that crop of golden curls, her 'butter wouldn't melt in the mouth' expression, and the way she looked at people in that coy way. Mick however, had got there first, mainly because he was twelve too, though he was not a looker. It hurt Tommy to know that Mick had achieved what he could only dream of.

Mick broke into his daydream.

'I shouldn't worry, she's just a hussy. C'mon we better get a move on or we won't get us tea.'

They broke into a trot, and at the bottom of the lane, turned right at the junction, passing in front of the village hall before arriving at the rickety, moss covered gate of Tommy's dad's house.

'See ya!' called Mick as he sped on round the corner to the garage where his father worked.

'I see you've been with that Mick again?' Tommy's father rasped in a disapproving tone, 'I've told you before that playing with that lout will do you no good. Can't you find someone your own age to do things with?'

'Like who?' replied Tommy hotly, 'Now Darren's gone, there's no one else round here that I can play with. And besides Mick knows an awful lot. He's teaching me about sex.'

'You what...?' His father laughed dryly before fuming at Tommy: 'What could he possibly teach you about sex, he probably doesn't know one end of a lass from the other.'

'He told me all about doing stuff with that Marion Smythe down the road,' Tommy insisted, then wished he hadn't said it as his dad went absolutely apoplectic.

'What the ...That's it!' He blazed 'You don't see that lout ever again. Do you hear me?'

Tommy ran out of the room and up to his bedroom.

He heard his father go out into the back garden and the squeak of the tool-shed door indicated that another digging session was about to commence. Soon he would smell the strong but sweet odour of '*Gold Block*' tobacco as his father lit up his pipe before commencing his weeding.

Since Mum died, Tommy had found it difficult having to communicate more with his father. His mother had been the most attentive. His dad was not the demonstrative type and had little in the way of 'bedside-manner' with kids. He now seemed grumpy and unapproachable. Tommy couldn't remember the last time his dad had so much as put a reassuring arm around him.

He often wondered whether his father's behaviour was the result of mum dying or whether it was just that people got grumpier as they got older. He definitely didn't remember him being quite that way before.

Tommy lay back on the bed, thinking about Marion and what Mick said he had been doing with her. He'd called her a hussy. What did that mean? What exactly did he do with Marion? He wondered. He knew that it involved the funny little thing between his legs, but what did one do with it? He wondered what Marion looked like without her knickers. He knew she wouldn't look like him down there, in fact if she were anything like what he'd seen of his mum in the bath, she wouldn't have much else either! He decided that he had so much more to ask Mick about.

Then he heard the squeak of the tool-shed door again and shortly after, the creaking treads of the staircase as his father climbed the stairs. He must have taken his boots off thought Tommy, he's awful quiet.

The bedroom door swung open and Tommy shrank back on his bed, convinced that his dad was about to continue his remonstration. But his dad appeared quiet, rubbing his stubbly chin with a dirt-laden hand, engrossed in thought. He padded over to the bed and sat at the foot.

'Now listen Tommy,' he began, 'I think, after what you said downstairs, it's time we had a little chat about sex.' He puffed several times on his pipe, pushing down the burnt tobacco with a calloused thumb. 'I don't want you gettin' all the wrong ideas from that lout down the road. If the truth was known he's probably tellin' you a pack of lies anyway and he'll get you into trouble, I swear. You'll find out later in life that there's folk who talk about things and there's folk that do them, an' those that do keep it to themselves. Mick's one of those that's *all* talk, so pay him no heed, alright?'

Tommy nodded, but was not of a mind to heed his dad.

'I'm going to tell you about sex, but I'm going to talk about how it happened between your mum and me, because you've got to understand the difference between smutty schoolboy sex and loving sex between two adult people, which was what your mum and me had.'

Tommy noticed that his father's eyes were glistening, tears forming along his lower eyelids, welling up then spilling in minute dollops to his cheeks below.

Tommy felt embarrassed. He knew his dad would find this conversation emotional. It was the first time he had ever seen his father tearful, and it disturbed him enormously. They never really talked about Mum but Tommy concluded that his dad must have loved his wife very much after all.

Suddenly he felt sorry for him. He moved across the bed and put an arm around his neck.

'Go on dad, yes, please tell me about it.' Now it was his turn to be tearful.

They sat there for a while, not speaking, while his father gathered his thoughts. It was the first time since his mum had died that Tommy had had a cuddle with his father. It felt good, and the heady perfume from the pipe tobacco mixed with his mild body odour seemed to enhance the experience, to eventually make it more memorable, perhaps.

'I remember when I first saw your mum, Tommy,' he began, 'she was beautiful – perhaps the most beautiful girl I had ever seen. She was slim with lily-white skin and faint freckles on her cheeks, golden, almost ginger hair and shining blue eyes.'

Tommy thought of Marion – his dad's description could have fitted her too and he felt the same about her.

'It was a few years before the war,' his dad continued, 'she had come round to ours with some potato peelings for the chickens. Her mother had sent her. I'd never clapped eyes on her before, probably because my dad thought the family was too hoity-toity for us farmers.'

'So why'd she bring the peelings?' Tommy asked.

'P'raps they felt sorry for us 'cos we was poor and thought we could do with 'em,' his Dad offered in reply.

'Anyhow, that's how it began. It was nearly harvest festival and the Vicar had been goin' round the village asking for people to give stuff to put on the altar. So I went round to see your mum - Agnes Cartwright as she was then - to ask her if she would like to come to the church with me to see the display before the service.'

'Did she say yes?' Tommy asked excitedly.

'Well, it was her mother who came to the door, an' she asked me what I wanted an' I asked if Agnes was in, an' her mother called to her old man. He said 'No, she's not in', but her mother said 'call again tomorrow', and I went home all upset.'

'Do you think she *was* in?' Tommy asked.

'I know she was. I saw her at the window when I left. She was peeping round the side of the curtain.'

'So what did you do?' Tommy was getting impatient.

'I did like she said – went round the next day – her father was at work and her mum let me into the house. So I asked her about the harvest festival and she said she'd like to.'

'And...?'

'And that was it. We went to the church and sat in the front pew, side by side, watching the Vicar arranging all the contributions on the alter table. After about 5 minutes I felt her hand in mine, it was amazing, I had never felt anything like it. It was as if an electric shock went up my arm. I remember thinking that this girl sitting bedside me was goin' to be mine and only mine.'

'You didn't fuck her then?' Tommy asked innocently.

Tommy's dad sat up with a jerk. 'Don't *ever* use that word, Tommy, it's not nice – no certainly not – do you know what it means?'

'Mick says he's done it to Marion and that I could too if she'll let me.'

'Well I've told you not to listen to Mick. I'll get to all that in good time, but first you've got to understand what loving someone is all about and how sex is a part of that.'

'How old were you then dad – when you asked Mum to the Harvest Festival?'

Tommy was anxious to see if there was any correlation with his own dilemma.

'Oh about 18…' Tommy's dad rubbed his swarthy chin trying to remember exactly. '…Just before my 19th birthday I think it was.'

Tommy was crestfallen. He would have to wait quite a long time, by the sound of it.

'I think I know how you felt Dad, I feel the same way about Marion, and now Mick doesn't want her no more, I think I'm going to ask her.'

His Dad looked down at him with a smile. 'But you're only nine lad, and you've got a lot more growin' up to do before you need to worry about girls – especially that one, 'cos she's three years older than you. She'll be lookin' at fifteen year- olds by now, I shouldn't wonder.'

It was late and they hadn't even had their tea yet. 'C'mon, Tommy, I'll tell you more about it as we have us tea,' and he got up off the bed and walked toward the door. 'What d'you fancy, a bit of cold pie or some spaghetti on toast?'

Tommy fancied cold pie. He liked to cover it in brown sauce.

He followed his father downstairs. He seemed to have built a bridge with him, but his dilemma over Marion was now of greater importance. It was chewing him up inside.

Over tea his father expanded on his theory of love and sex in the context of his relationship with Agnes Cartwright. Despite the discussion being particular rather than generic, Tommy found parallels with his own dilemma and solutions too, which might similarly work for him.

Tommy's searching questions necessitated explicit answers from his father, to the extent that he was clearly embarrassed as he gave his replies. Nonetheless, he didn't shirk a single one, despite his never having experienced some of the activities that Mick had apparently discussed with Tommy.

Armed with this new information Tommy decided he would talk to Marion but he also vowed to test out just how experienced Mick actually was.

After eating supper, his father reached again for his pipe, knocked out the ash on the side of the hearth and refilled it with fresh tobacco. 'OK, Tommy,' he began, applying a match to the bowl and puffing upon the stem until the pipe was properly alight. 'I think it's time you went up to bed. You'd better have a wash and put your dirty clothes in the tub to soak. There's some hot water in the kettle on the stove.'

The next morning Tommy awoke at the call of his father from the kitchen below. He felt elated, particularly over his new relationship with his dad, but it soon turned to despondency when it dawned on him that it was Monday – school day.

He dressed and went down for his breakfast.

As he ate his porridge, idly stirring it around the rim of the bowl with his spoon, he tried to set out in his mind how he was going to tackle Marion. It really depended on whether Mick was true to his word and would actually drop her like a hot brick. He would have to wait and see. Then there was the second task of testing out Mick himself and determining just how right his Dad might be.

He had compiled in his mind some questions, based on what his dad had told him during the 'little chat.' Tommy decided that he would not be a friend of Mick any longer if it proved that his dad was right about him.

'Come on, eat up,' his dad called out from the scullery, as he pulled on his boots, the dry clods of mud from yesterday's digging dropping onto the clay tiled floor, 'you'll be late for school if you don't watch it.'

Tommy swallowed the last spoonful of porridge and grabbed his satchel. 'I need a shilling for me lunch Dad,' he called back, waiting at the door.

'Tell 'em you'll give it to them on Friday, after I've been to the Post Office, now go on be off with you.'

Tommy sighed. He hated having to tell the teacher he didn't have his lunch-money. She always singled him out by drawing it to the attention of the rest of the class, following which the jibes would come from the other boys in the playground afterwards. They would call out their nasty little rhymes like 'Poor little slob, Tommy no bob' and others that equally portrayed his plight.

He shuffled out of the house and head bowed, walked slowly down the path to the gate. Mick was waiting for him behind the hedge.

'Bloody Hell Tommy! What's the matter wi' you? You look like you've got ill wi' summat.'

'Been having sex lessons wi' me Dad.' Tommy replied curtly, watching Mick's face intently. He decided that if he saw any sign of embarrassment in those eyes he would know that Mick had been lying yesterday.

But there was nothing but Mick's blank stare. Then his face cracked and he exploded in laughter.

'You what? Your Dad gave you a talk about the birds and the bees? What did he tell yer?'

'That's for me to know and you to find out,' replied Tommy triumphantly. He felt he now had the upper hand so he walked off down the road towards the school.

Mick caught up with him and grabbed his sleeve.

'Hang on mate,' he spluttered, 'you've gotta tell me.'

Tommy ignored him and continued walking at a slightly increased pace.

'I don't have to tell you nothing, seeing as you know it all already, or so you say.'

The pair walked on, conversation over for the moment. Mick realised that Tommy wasn't going to tell him anything and it was making him mad.

Just before they got to the school gate, Tommy turned and faced Mick. 'What are you goin' to do about Marion?' he asked.

'Oh fuck Marion, I'm not seeing her no more,' he replied. 'But I don't want you askin' her about what we did the other day OK?'

'So, it didn't really happen then?' Tommy quizzed.

'Well, maybe I was exaggeratin' a bit, but she was definitely doin' things…to begin with anyway.' Mick asserted.

The two boys went their separate ways, Tommy to his 2nd Year classroom and Mick to his in the 4th Form at the back of the building. Mick was in his last term at Ardingly Village School before he would transfer to the Jessie Grey School in Haywards Heath in the September, as would Marion.

Tommy realised he would have to move fast if he was to make any inroads into his planned relationship with her. He would have to tackle her at the morning break in the playground today, but he put his fear and trepidation to one side for the moment to concentrate on his first lesson - geography.

It was all about rivers. Their sources, how slow or fast they flowed over their passage to the sea, something about torrents, rapids, meandering, horseshoe lakes, tributaries and deltas. Tommy couldn't quite take it all in but the teacher had given him a fact sheet to study for homework. Tommy had to find a river on the map and explain in a short essay, what might be found at various stages on its route to the sea. He thought he might need his Dad's help on that.

He looked anxiously at the clock – nearly twenty to eleven. The bell for break would ring any minute. He galvanised himself in preparation for his showdown with Marion.

In a way he hoped the bell wouldn't ring, in fact the longer it took the more nervous he became, until he found himself inwardly saying that he didn't have to do this, why not just forget about her. But then the picture of her face appeared in his mind and he found a little more strength to carry out the endeavour. He realised that if he didn't, he might regret it for the rest of his life.

The shrill jangling sound of the headmistress's hand-bell in the playground made him jump and in one swift motion, the 28 pupils in the room swarmed around the classroom door.

Out in the playground Tommy looked around for Marion. At first he thought she must have stayed inside, probably talking to that Priscilla Smith. She was always going about with her. They sat next to each other in class and helped each other with their lessons, and often held hands. How Tommy would have liked to do the same.

He was about to give up looking when he saw the two girls leaving the toilets at the back of the playground. They were both sniggering about something. Tommy quietly walked a bit nearer to eavesdrop on their discussion.

It was about boys, as usual. Marion was expounding on her adventures with various boys in the school, and those whom she might tackle next. Tommy was disappointed to note that every boy mentioned was at least eleven but what he found most intriguing was the number of boys that Marion said she had kissed. Twelve, she had said to Pricilla. That, he thought, was disgusting. It showed that she was a bit of a flirt. Perhaps that was what Mick meant when he called her a 'hussy'. Tommy got a bit closer, to find out more.

'That Mick was terrible,' Marion was saying to her friend, 'his hands were all over me the other day, and he'd only just stopped going round with that Claire Williams. She was sick of him too. Do you know, I had to slap his face to get him to stop mauling me. I really don't know why I bothered with him. He even tried to get his hand in my knickers, so that was the end, I just ran away from him. I don't ever want to see his spotty face again!'

Priscilla's laugh was a mixture of mirth and embarrassment. She hadn't actually plucked up the courage to 'court' any of the boys in her class yet. She was learning from her friend, but she was the shy type, so it would be some time before she would reach the giddy heights of Marion's sexual awareness and be able to act upon it.

Tommy felt let down. Clearly Mick was a liar and a fantasist. But Marion was not the sort he thought she would be either. He realised too that if he carried out his quest, and if she accepted, he too would just become a statistic in her love life, to be scorned or laughed at by Marion and her girlfriends.

Downcast, he decided there and then that he would abort his mission and go back to the classroom to wait for the bell.

1956

A canine companion

It was Saturday morning. Tommy was up early. He could always find the energy to get out of bed when it was not a school day.

He dressed quickly and rushed downstairs to get his breakfast. His dad was already at the table pouring himself his second mug of tea.

'There's porridge on the stove Tommy, help yerself,' he said.

Tommy took the wooden spoon and lifted a dollop of the stiff, lumpy substance, dropped it into a bowl, then drowned it in milk from the pitcher. As he walked back to the table he glanced out of the window towards the cabbage patch.

'Dad...dad, there's a dog in the cabbages. It's diggin' them up or summat.'

Tommy's dad shot up out of his chair, cursing, and rushed for the door, with Tommy following close behind.

As they approached the cabbage patch, the dog looked up and ran over to them wagging its tail furiously.

'There's no collar on 'im, lad,' his dad ascertained, running his fingers through the course hair about the dog's neck, 'must be a stray I should think.'

The dog meanwhile was licking a couple of scratches on Tommy's shin.

'I think he likes me, dad. If he's a stray does that mean we can keep him?'

'Nay lad, at least, not until we've reported him and no one's claimed him. We'll lock 'im in the shed, then go to the police station. Now go back in and finish your porridge first.'

Tommy rushed back into the house. He dearly hoped no one would claim the black, woolly terrier and he wolfed down his breakfast as fast as he could manage.

At the Police Station, the news was more positive. The sergeant listened to Tommy's dad's description of the dog and frowned, rubbing the back of his neck and looking skyward.

'I can't recollect ever seeing a dog like that in Ardingly,' he sighed eventually, 'mebbe I should phone through to Wakehurst an' see if they can help.'

Tommy was first elated then finally disappointed. That the dog had travelled a couple of miles was feasible but he hoped remote.

'Why don't you look after him for a few days while we look for his owner. Then, if we don't get anyone claiming him you can keep him.'

That was music to Tommy's ears and he jumped up and down excitedly.

On the way home his dad asked what he would call the dog.

'He's goin' to be called Rufus,' said Tommy firmly.

Three weeks later, a black Wolseley 6/80 with a lit up sign on the roof saying 'Police' drew up outside Tommy's dad's house.

A rather stern looking policeman alighted from the car, adjusted his trousers and checked his notebook, then looked up toward the front door.

Tommy shrank back behind the curtain, worried. They were going to take Rufus back, he thought.

'The police are here dad', Tommy whispered, all apprehensive. 'He's comin' up the path now.'

The knock was firm and hard and Tommy's dad jumped out of his chair and strode swiftly to the door.

'Mr Norton?' enquired the policeman.

'That's me.'

'I'm from the station at Wakehurst. It's about the stray you reported. Your own station here in Ardingly passed it on to us...'

'Has no one claimed it?' interrupted Tommy.

'No lad, they haven't, so it looks like he's yours now, but you'll have to go to the post office and get a licence for it.'

'How much will that cost?' asked Tommy, alarmed.

'I think it's seven shillings and sixpence ha'penny' replied the policeman, 'but check at the post office.'

Tommy's dad frowned and ran his fingers through his thin hair.

'Thank you officer, we'll get it sorted as soon as we can, but I'm a bit busy at the moment, what with the vegetable garden and us two bein' on our own.'

'So you'll have him then – the dog?'

'Yes, I suppose we will. Tommy will be right disappointed if I said 'No' wouldn't you son?'

Tommy nodded enthusiastically.

'Then I'll be off,' said the policeman with wave and he showed himself out.

'Now listen Tommy,' his dad began, 'we ain't got money to burn and seven shillings and sixpence ha'penny takes a lot of savin' up for. So we won't be able to get the licence straight away. But you mustn't let on to other people that we ain't got it yet, OK?'

Tommy didn't care about that. He was just over the moon that the dog was now theirs for good.

'OK Dad, I won't say nowt but we'll have to get him a collar with his name on.'

Tommy's dad scratched his head while he thought about that.

'Tell you what Tommy, I've got that old broken leather belt upstairs. Mebbe I could make a collar out of it an' put a name on it. That'd do wouldn't it – for now at least.'

Tommy thought so too, then rushed out to the yard to give his new dog a hug.

1958

Anxiety

Mr Robertson, the year 4 form teacher wrote a short sentence on the dusty blackboard:
'Year 4 pupils: Headmistress, Mrs Alderman will give a talk after break. 11 o'clock prompt.'

He turned to face the class and for a few seconds, cast his eyes over the rows of expectant faces. 'Right you lot,' he started with a grin, 'this is the last time you'll see my ugly face for some time, if not forever.'
He waited for the muted 'hoorays' to die down before continuing:
'Now you may think that's of great benefit to you but think on: Summer holidays start as of this afternoon and then in September you will find out what real schoolwork is all about. It won't be like here, where I have had the dubious privilege of teaching you everything I know. You'll have a different teacher for each subject when you get to Jesse Grey and they're not all nice and forgiving like me, so woe betide you! Especially you, Richard Albright, they'll take none of your nonsense there. You'll likely get caned day in and day out.'
Albright shrugged his shoulders, spat out his chewing gum and stuck it in the inkwell at the corner of his desk then pulled an ugly face at the teacher.

Tommy felt his heart in his mouth. He hadn't had a good year so far. He had come second to last in the end of term tests and both the headmistress and his dad had been extremely disappointed. From what Mr Robertson said, it sounded very much as if he would not survive the coming years at the Jesse Grey Secondary School. He hoped that he could prevent the thought of it spoiling his summer holiday.

After 'Break', at precisely eleven o'clock, Mrs Alderman was at Mr. Robertson's desk in front of perhaps two thirds of the class.

She paced across the room and back, waiting for the dawdlers before commencing her announcement.

Tommy felt embarrassed, for he knew that Mr. Robertson commanded little respect from some of his pupils and this delay was no doubt a demonstration of that. However, Mrs. Alderman was made of sterner stuff.

'Right, I'm going to start now,' she said pointing to the writing on the blackboard, 'and any pupil not here will stay behind after school this afternoon and complete two hours of detention.'

Tommy looked out of the window overlooking the playground and sports field. He could see some of his fellow pupils kicking a ball about on the grass, but he could do little about warning them.

Then he had an idea and he put up his hand.

'Yes Tommy, what is it?'

'Should I go outside and get the others, Miss? I don't think Mr Robertson explained very well that *everyone* had to attend.'

'Yes, Tommy, do that and tell them that if they are not sitting at their desks within five minutes, they won't be going home at lunchtime.'

But of course it didn't work. It was the last day of term and no one would be coming back to Ardingly Primary School, so how could any teacher maintain authority over a bunch of errant school leavers?

Tommy went back to the classroom with his tail between his legs. He would have to explain why they wouldn't come. He couldn't repeat to Mrs Alderman what some of the boys had said, it was too rude. And besides, they said, they would be breaking up at lunchtime, so there was no point.

'They're not comin' back Miss,' Tommy hesitated before continuing, 'they told me to tell you to go and…you know.'

'No, I don't know, actually,' spat Mrs Alderman, her face black with rage. She snatched up the board rubber, turned to the blackboard and furiously rubbed out the message that Mr Robertson had written. She was positively shaking.

'This talk was to help you find your way at Jesse Grey, but you'll all have to do it by yourselves now,' she stammered, gathering up her papers. 'Best of luck with that!' And she stormed out.

Tommy was already quite apprehensive about starting at Jesse Grey, but the episode with Mrs Alderman heightened his concern. He could have well done with that advice of hers, he thought.

1959

Sorrow

It was a Thursday. Tommy arrived home from school and threw his satchel on the kitchen table ready for doing his homework. Usually his father would be in the snug at that time, having his afternoon cup of tea. But the snug was empty and there was no sign of him, either upstairs or down. He's probably out, down the shop, he thought as he settled at the table and commenced his mathematics.

Tommy was not too hot on mathematics and it soon became apparent that he needed his dad to help with the harder questions. He'd been gone more than half an hour and that seemed unusual.

Tommy went out through the scullery into the garden. He looked around the vegetable patch, hoping to see his dad hoeing the weeds or planting a row of cabbages or the like. But there was just an eerie silence, save for the occasional tweet of a bird and the buzz of the bees as they flitted from bloom to bloom on the runner beans.

Tommy walked farther down the narrow garden path toward the fruit bushes. His eyes came to rest upon a pair of boots protruding from the tall stalks of rhubarb at the end of the garden. Squinting against the light of the sun he could just make out a trouser leg but the umbrella-like leaves hid any further detail.

Tommy knew there was something wrong, even before he rushed over to the rhubarb. He felt his heart pounding in his chest as he ran. All sorts of lurid pictures of what might have befallen his father flashed through his mind and he tried desperately to push them aside. Yet he knew this was something serious.

'Dad, Dad, what's up?' he asked anxiously as he arrived at the scene. His father was face down in the patch, not moving, his cap lying upturned in the mud, his hair matted with sweat.

Tommy placed his hand on the nape of his father's neck. It felt cold and clammy. The handle of his spade protruded from beneath his rough jacket, his hand still clinging to it and in the other, his beloved pipe, its stem stuck firmly in the soil.

Tommy knew he was dead. He didn't need to make any further checks. He just sat there, his head on his dad's shoulder, sobbing his heart out.

Eventually he realised he had to do something. He wasn't sure what, but maybe the doctor would know what to do, even though he would not be able to save him.

He lifted his father's head and placed his cap beneath it, protecting his face from the mud then rushed off out of the gate and down past the bakery to the doctor's house.

Dr Snelling's wife, Mary, heard him coming up the path and she lifted her ruddy-cheeked face from her weeding amongst the roses.

'Why Tommy, you look all hot and bothered. Is something the matter?'

'Me dad's dead,' Tommy wheezed tearfully, all out of breath, 'I need the doctor to come an' help me.'

Mrs Snelling leaned on her trowel and stood up, wiping her muddy hands on her apron, a look of disbelief across her crimson face. 'Surely not lad, I only saw him not a couple of hours ago, going for his tobacco.'

'Well he's definitely dead now, Mrs Snelling, he's in the garden, flat on his tummy.'

Mrs Snelling took Tommy by the arm and led him into the house. She knocked on the door to the surgery. 'Wait here Tommy, I'll get him, he'll no doubt have a patient with him at the moment.' And she opened the door, slid in quietly and shut it behind her.

Tommy could hear a brief conversation behind the door but couldn't quite make out what was being said. After a short period, but what seemed an eternity to Tommy, the door opened and Dr Snelling filled the frame, his black leather bag at his side.

'Come on then young Tom, let's go and see what we can do.' He said in his kindliest voice. 'Mary, call the ambulance please.'

On the way he asked Tommy a whole series of questions, like 'What time did he discover his dad?' And 'What had he planned to do today.' And 'Had he been taking his pills regularly?'

Tommy couldn't answer the latter question. He didn't even know his dad was taking any.

'What did he have wrong with 'im?' Tommy enquired with a good deal of concern.

'He suffered from angina, your dad, but not too seriously,' Dr Snelling said, 'do you know what that is?'

Tommy didn't really know, though he had heard the word before.

'Summat to do with your heart, I think, isn't it?' He offered. 'He always got out of breath if he did a lot of diggin'.'

'That's right Tommy, so the tablets countered that by helping to keep his heart right. Maybe he'd been forgetting to take them, we'll see.'

Dr Snelling realised that if it were true, there was not a lot he could do for the father. His biggest concern now was Tommy and what would happen to him? He had no other family. His mother was dead, his father, an only child, had lost both parents in the zeppelin bombing of London in 1915 while they were visiting relations. There was no one to take care of Tommy now. He looked down with pity at the glum face walking beside him. 'Be brave Tommy, we'll sort this out together, eh?'

Tommy looked up at the doctor's craggy face and through his tears he saw his reassuring smile.

'I'll be all right, Doctor Snelling, I'm nearly thirteen. I can take care of myself.'

'I'm sure you can lad,' the doctor agreed. 'But I think it best if maybe you were to stay at our house for a bit. My Mary will look after you, after all, you can't cook your own meals, can you?'

The sudden realisation that he was alone in the world hit Tommy with a wallop. He had no money, no family to call upon for support, and although he was nearly thirteen, the thought of going back to his house, without his dad, scared him.

'Shall I pack a few things an' bring 'em over? he asked.

'Yes lad, do it now, then we'll have our tea,' Doctor Snelling agreed, patting him gently on the shoulder.

'Should I bring Rufus?'
'Of course you should, we can't leave him to starve, can we?'

1961

Tranquillity

Life with the Snellings was rapidly healing the hurt inside Tommy following his father's death. It turned out that nicotine poisoning had been the cause of his demise. He had apparently sucked on his pipe for some time after it had been extinguished, swallowing the nicotine-laden juices produced.

Mrs Snelling had never had children but it was clear to Tommy that had she done so, she would have been a wonderful mother, for she treated him like her own, always fussing over him and making sure he had the best of everything.

For the first time in his short life Tommy felt relaxed, happy and confident.

It was the year that John Kennedy was elected President of the USA, and one April afternoon Tommy sat glued to the television. It was exciting stuff. According to the newsreader, the Russians had put a man into orbit in a spaceship. An astronaut called Yuri Gagarin. Tommy was hoping that there would be some pictures but the newsreader just handed over to another correspondent.

He turned off the television and returned to his revision for his mock 'O level' exams, which were fast approaching. His schoolwork had improved somewhat over his last two or three terms. Mr

Snelling was very proud to read the headmaster's comment at the end of the last term:

'Tommy has come on in leaps and strides this term. Let's hope his high standard of work continues.'

Tommy had never been very academic, but now, with Dr Snelling's knowledge and assistance, he suddenly found his studies interesting.

As he was working out his quadratic equations, he suddenly found himself thinking of his long lost love Marion Smythe. Since he'd been at the Jesse Grey School he hadn't ever seen her. That was not really surprising because it was a big school and she would be three years ahead of him at least. He might not even recognise her now and she could even have left the school anyway.

He wondered whether he would ever have a girlfriend as pretty as she had been.

Eventually his mock exams were upon him. For the first time in his life Tommy felt confident that he'd do well. He had discovered that the secret to exams was to do the required amount of revision – a little each day, rather than leaving it all till the last moment and rushing it. He sat in the exam room each day, writing furiously as all around him sat with their pens in their mouths and their eyes looking skyward.

When the results were announced, it was no surprise to Tommy that he'd passed every subject.

Dr and Mrs Snelling were so overjoyed at his success that they swanked about it to the neighbours for days, only refraining when the butcher told Mrs Snelling that the proof of the pudding would be the proper GCE's at the end of term. She came back home with her tail between her legs that day.

'Cheeky so-and-so that butcher', she muttered at Dr Snelling. 'If there was another in the village I'd stop buying from him. Did you hear what he said to me?'

Dr Snelling hadn't been there, so of course, no, he didn't hear. Nonetheless he listened carefully and nodded agreement at the end of her rant.

'We'll wait for the real results, then we'll show them,' he replied with a smile.

Mrs Snelling took her meat out of the shopping basket, slapped in on the draining board then slipped on her apron and began to prepare the supper.

1962

Pride

'How many subjects are they letting you take Tom,' Roger asked, as he studied the circular issued by the headmaster to every 5th Form pupil in the school.

'I dunno yet,' Tommy replied, 'Hoppity says that as I did OK in the mocks, I should take at least five and he reckons I'd probably pass Maths, General Science, Geography, History and English. He reckoned I might even get French too, but I'm not sure.'

'Hoppity' was the form teacher, so nicknamed because he was injured during the first war and his left leg was a little stiffer and shorter than his right, making him give a sort of double hop with each stride. Naturally no one mentioned that name to his face. His actual name was, by some coincidence, George Hopkins.

Roger thought for a moment, then came up with his decision. 'I'm going to take all eleven of them. That way I've got the best chance of getting something.'

'I don't think that's good logic,' said Tommy, 'You'll have to do so much revision and you won't have the time to cover everything.'

'Well my dad says that the GCE. exams are a lot easier than the Matriculation in his day, when you had to pass everything to get a certificate. He reckons I should take them all.'

Tommy was not inclined to argue. 'OK, tell you what, so will I and we'll have a bet.' he said.

'What sort of bet?'

'That I get more subjects than you.'

'How much?'

'Ten shillings!'

'Blimey! Ten shillings?'

'Yes, we've got to make it worth it.'

'OK, you're on.' Roger spat on the palm of his hand and offered it to Tommy who did the same. They shook hands vigorously, then wiped their damp hands on the side of their trousers.

'But it's a lot of money, ten shillings,' Roger suddenly said, almost as if he was going to renege on the agreement.

'Well, you better start saving straight away,' Tommy sniggered, 'we'll go and fill out the applications now.'

1965

Joy and Despair in equal measure.

It was Monday, and although it was only November, it was already snowing after an appalling summer. It was cold enough to settle and the beginnings of a smooth blanket of white spread across the grassy bank opposite the college, punctuated here and there with irregular circles where the trees sheltered the grass from the heavy fall.

Tommy marched quickly across the gravel toward the students hall of residence, his footprints the first to spoil the fresh snow. He balanced his satchel over his head in order to keep the falling crystals off his hair, so avoiding them melting and running down his neck. Lectures were over for the day and he looked forward to a quiet evening in the college bar after dinner.

It was his first term at Durham, not his first choice of University, but having failed his interview for Cambridge, it seemed the next best thing at the time. It was his headmaster's recommendation. He had advised Tommy that Durham was the third most sought after university, and that it was actually better academically in some areas. He would not be disappointed.
Tommy had made the decision himself, as Dr Snelling had said he was now old enough to decide his own future.
He had sunk all his energy into his schoolwork, for he had decided that he would try to make something of

himself. He had no desire to end up working the land as his father had expected. He wanted to become an entrepreneur or perhaps a scientist of some kind.

After sailing through his 'O' levels, gaining every one he had taken and ten shillings into the bargain, he had decided to study the sciences at 'A' level. His grades were high enough to enrol at any University of his choosing, but he knew the interview might let him down. He was, after all, a farmer's son, and had the rugged, rather swarthy look of a land-worker. Not the sort of material those Oxbridge universities sought in large numbers.

Although he had only been at Durham a short time, he had already discovered that elements of his life there would be purgatory indeed. He would never get fat, however little he exercised, because most of the food served up in the canteen was inedible, even by his own limited culinary experience.

He would never get enough sleep, because the subjects he had chosen meant a high proportion of self-study.

On top of that, there was the time spent upon the mandatory social life without which a well-rounded university education was unachievable. After all, there was no doubt that this latter aspect contributed greatly towards moulding the student into the intelligent, self-assured, gregarious yet sophisticated being that would walk tall in life.

He was sitting alone in the canteen, tackling what was purported to be a portion of cheese pie and peas. He was deep in thought, twisting the stringy cheesy crust around his fork when a rather good looking, somewhat older girl put her tray on the table opposite him and asked if he minded.

'Not at all,' Tommy replied, staring intently at her face. He determined that she was attractive rather than pretty. She was also fairly busty but not over-weight, with an endearing smile.

She sat down and started to eat.

'You one of the freshers?' she enquired, her mouth full.

'Yeah! I started this term,' Tommy began, 'tried to get into Cambridge, but failed, so this is the next best thing apparently.'

'You must be kidding!' The girl replied, 'Nothing like. This is my last year, thank God, providing I get my law degree, but I might have to stay another year if I decide to do a post grad in Corporate Law.'

'I'm doing Biosciences - a four-year course. I'm Tommy, what's your name?'

'Marion,' she replied, but without further details.

Tommy's heart flipped. He could see it now…The resemblance, that face, the golden curls of his lost love.

'Not Marion Smythe by any chance?' He asked, his eyes shining with emotion.

'The very one,' she replied, 'should I know you?'

'Probably not,' Tommy sounded downcast. 'I did try to speak to you once a long time ago, when we lived in Ardingly. You were my idol in those days, but I was only nine at the time and you were twelve, so I had no chance.'

'Well to answer your question, I s'pose at that age 3 years makes a difference' she replied, with not so much as an exclamation at the coincidence, 'after all it's 33% of your life, but the percentage gets smaller as one gets older. I would consider any boy from any year at Uni...if I liked them enough.'

Tommy felt his heart soar, the thumping in his chest seemed to him to be audible to all in the dining hall. He now knew he had a good chance of finally realising his boyhood dream.

'So I'm in with a chance then?' he asked, echoing his thoughts, and without waiting for her to empty her mouth, he added 'could I offer you a pub dinner one day next week?'

'Don't see why not, we are already acquainted by the sound of it. So yes, I think we could do that.'

'I'm not treading on someone else's toes am I?' he asked.

'Not at the moment, no, I'm what you might call 'in between' boyfriends currently.'

Tommy slumped back on the bench and just stared at her, smiling. It had been that easy he couldn't believe it. After all these years!

He ate no more of his cheese pie. Instead, he gathered everything onto his tray and stood up.

'Right then, I'll give you a shout on Wednesday if that's alright, about seven?'

'OK!'

He was about to leave when he remembered that he hadn't asked where he was to pick her up. 'By the way, where will I find you?'

'I'll meet you here if you like.' Marion replied.

'OK. See you then, if not in the bar later tonight perhaps?'

Marion smiled sweetly. 'Perhaps,' she replied before shovelling in another mouthful.

Tommy took his tray over to the rack and sauntered out of the dining hall, a sudden skip in his step.

Outside, the snow had been falling steadily and was now some two or three inches deep. The gravel was now a quagmire of slush from the many footprints of students passing back and forth. Tommy slipped and slithered his way back to his room to get an hour or so's studying under his belt before going for a beer and hopefully, another chance meeting with Marion.

On the staircase up to his room he bumped into David Benson, the first person he had befriended on arrival at the college. It was the duty of the second year students to show the freshers around the campus in their first week and David had been given Tommy as his protégé.

'Just going over to the bar, Tom,' he called 'are you coming over?'

'Maybe in a while,' Tommy replied, 'I've got a bit of work to do first, then I might, because I'm hoping that Marion Smythe will be there. I sat with her at supper tonight. We went to the same primary school. Strange coincidence eh?'

'Rather you than me, mate' David whispered under his breath, but not quite quietly enough.

'Why do you say that?' Tommy queried.

David blushed. He hadn't intended Tommy to hear his comment.

'Look, I don't know whether you know this, but she's reputed to be the college bicycle, probably been with just about every bloke in the place, she flits from one unsuspecting victim to another like a rabbit on heat. If you do get it together, don't expect it to last more than a week. The first you'll know about being dropped is when you'll see her on the arm of the next guy. Ask anyone, they'll all tell you the same.'

Tommy was dumbstruck. In five seconds flat his emotions had shot from elation to despair.

Could Marion really be that bad, he wondered. He cast his mind back to those earlier school days and the conversation he overheard between Marion and her friend, Priscilla Smith. She seemed pretty wayward in those days too, so maybe a leopard cannot change its spots. But would he be able to stop her run of admirers and hold on to her for the duration of her studies at Durham? He didn't know, but he knew that he had to try. After all it had been nigh on ten years that he'd harboured this lust for her.

He decided he'd take no notice of David and just see how far he could get.

A couple of hours later in 1965

Passion

Tommy completed his self-imposed hour's work and then brushed his teeth and changed into a fresh pullover. He ran a comb through his shock of wavy, light brown hair, trying to get it into some form of control then made for the door. He didn't want to be late in case he missed Marion.

As he trudged through the snow for a second time that day, he thought about his Wednesday date and where he might take her. It couldn't be too expensive, especially if she would expect him to pay, but maybe being both students, she would cough up her share? He didn't know. Cross that bridge when I come to it, he thought.

He'd heard that the Shakespeare in Saddler Street was a good traditional pub, so maybe they could get a drink there then get a takeaway or something afterwards. That might be more affordable. He decided he'd discuss it with her when he got to the college bar.

Pushing his way through a sizeable crowd of drinkers gathered near the bar entrance, he made his way across the room, casting his eyes around the various groups of students, looking to see if Marion was about. Given that she had a reputation, he feared that she would be there somewhere with a crowd of admirers surrounding her, all vying for her attention. But no, she hadn't shown yet. He ordered a beer and leaning back on the bar, fixed his eyes on the doorway, waiting for her to arrive.

By ten o'clock he was still waiting and his pint was finished. Now he was in a bit of a quandary. He had brought only enough money for two drinks, one of which was for her. If she didn't show, he could have another. But what if he bought himself another and then by some unlucky chance she arrived?

He decided not to bother worrying about it and just go back to his room. He was seeing her on Wednesday anyway, so tonight wasn't really that important.

He left the bar and was just walking out into the snow when he literally bumped into her as she skipped over the puddles of melted snow. Steadying her as she almost lost her balance, he held on to her until she was fully in control again. It was the closest he had been to her and he could smell the light, sweet odour of her cheap perfume and feel the firm flesh of her arms through her anorak.

'What's it like in there?' she asked. 'Full as usual, no doubt.'

'Yes, pretty much,' he replied.

'Tell you what, I've got half a bottle of gin in my room – nicked it from my dad's drinks cabinet during the hols. Fancy coming up for a swig or two? Might be better than fighting your way to the bar in there.'

That was a bit forward, thought Tommy, suddenly feeling apprehensive. He thought back to what Dave Benson had said of her. Was she setting him up as her next victim? Might be best not to accept at this early stage he decided.

'That's nice of you, but one glass might lead to another, and I've got to finish an essay before tomorrow,' he lied.

But then she pulled such a miserable expression.

'Oh God! I've done it again haven't I,' she suggested, 'given you the wrong impression. Seems to be a habit of mine. Just come up for one drink and we'll talk about old times in Ardingly or something. You can go and finish your essay after.'

Tommy still felt that he was being enticed, but perhaps less so, so he caved in.

'OK, just the one,' he replied.

She smiled, grabbed his arm, and led him back to her room.

'I'm on the second floor,' she added as they entered the building.

Tommy noticed that her room well reflected the fact that she had been at college for some time. It was full of knick-knacks and the walls had lots of posters of local and college events, but Tommy was most surprised by the myriad of newspaper cuttings and pictures of James Dean splattered all around the mirror by the washbasin.

'My idol, shame he's gone.' she volunteered as she dug out the gin bottle from the cupboard.

'So, I was *your* idol at primary school, was I?' she teased. 'Funny that you never talked to me.'

'I couldn't pluck up the courage,' Tommy replied, 'besides, you were apparently going out with my mate Mick. God knows why.'

'You must be kidding. He was an absolute heathen. I dropped him as soon as I found out. I really don't know why I bothered, but at that age I suppose I was glad of the attention.'

'And now?'

'Well, I do tend to put it about a bit, but how else can I find someone I really want to spend my life with?'

Tommy's heart skipped a beat. So there was method in her madness, he ventured.

Marion passed him a tooth-mug half full of gin with an apology.

'Sorry, I don't have any other glasses, but it's clean.' Then she took a swig out of the bottle and sat on the bed.

'Come and sit over here, that folding chair isn't comfortable,' she said.

Tommy complied and took a sip from his glass.

'Sorry there's no tonic, but I've got some orange you could mix with it, if you like?'

Tommy didn't like, and downed the rest of the gin so that he could get rid of the tooth-mug, which was proving difficult to hold without spilling as the soft mattress jogged about.

'So how do you feel about me now, after all this time?' Marion asked, rather provocatively.

Tommy was all of a fluster. He wasn't sure quite how to answer. He decided to just tell the truth.

'Well, not having taken the opportunity at primary school, it's been chewing me up ever since, to be honest' he replied, looking directly into her eyes.

'Oh, for God's sake, come here,' she whispered, wrapping her arms around him and drawing him closer. And she kissed him full on the lips.

'I never even knew.'

'Well, you wouldn't would you, I was only nine at the time and you were twelve, which was so much older.'

She hugged him tighter. 'You're three years younger than I am now too, but I don't care and I really like you. I know you've got an essay to do, but do you want to stay here tonight?' she asked.

'I lied about the essay,' he admitted, 'I felt I might be getting in too deep at an early stage otherwise.'

'That's just plain silly, you should always go with the flow. How else can things take their natural course? That settles it – you're staying. It's late now so let's get into bed and get warm.'

Even if he'd wanted to, Tommy couldn't have thought of a way out.

He was in paradise.

A week later in 1965

Disgust then delight

Tommy felt his life had taken a turn for the better. He was in love. He'd spent practically all his free time with Marion. Every day over the last week they had eaten together, been for long walks down by the river together and slept together every evening in her room. He adored her. And she reciprocated, even to the extent of making plans for the holidays at the end of term.

She was his first sexual encounter, but it was clear to him that she was far more experienced, even sex mad, he determined. But he didn't care. He was in paradise and loving every minute of it.

When he was alone he found himself unable to concentrate on his studies. She was always on his mind.

So he was shocked that Sunday evening, when he walked into the college bar to find Marion amongst a group of students, sitting in the lap of the rowing team captain, one of the third year students, with her arm around his neck.

She looked up and saw Tommy, but didn't acknowledge him. Instead she lowered her eyes and rested her head on the rower's shoulder.

Tommy was mortified. He froze on the spot, trying to figure out his next move. He knew that if he went over to her there would be an embarrassing exchange, yet he didn't want to give her the impression he didn't care. Equally if he walked out, she would feel she had won.

He looked around the room. Perhaps the best option was to test Marion a little further by ignoring her.

Paula Dixon, a first year student also studying Biosciences was at the bar getting a drink. Tommy walked over to her. Paula was quite the opposite of Marion. She was medium height, slight of build, her hair was dark, almost black, and her skin lightly tanned. Her deep brown eyes shone under the bar lights.

He offered to buy the drink for her, which she gratefully accepted then he ordered a beer for himself. The pair found an empty table and sat down.

'I thought you and Marion were an item?' She queried, not mincing her words as she took a sip from her glass.

Tommy was surprised she had noticed.

'Well, I thought we were, sort of,' he replied, 'but I believe she likes to keep things a little loose, or so I'm told.'

'Yeah, I've heard.' Paula replied with an edge in her voice. She looked across at Marion, who was squirming around in the rower's lap.

Tommy was getting annoyed. It seemed to him that everyone knew what Marion was like. He felt that the whole college was perhaps waiting with bated breath to see how his relationship would end up.

Well, they won't get the satisfaction, he thought.

He turned to Paula. 'So how are you getting on with your studies – quite a lot of work isn't it?'

'Yeah, but I'm enjoying it. Probably because it runs in the family a bit, 'cos my dad is a virologist and my mum is a botanist so I picked up a lot of that stuff from them. What's your dad do?'

'He died a few years ago, and my mum passed on when I was about four. He was a farmer, or should I say a smallholder. We were pretty poor really.'

'Oh, my God! How awful for you, how did you cope?

'I had nice neighbours. The local doctor and his wife.'

'What? Did they adopt you then?'

'Well, sort of. I was about thirteen at the time my dad died and they took me in, with my dog, to live with them.'

'Didn't they have to formally adopt you?'

'I don't know, I never asked. I do remember someone coming to the house to talk to them about me, but I was given ten shillings and told to go to the cinema. When I came back, nothing was said and I didn't ask as I was afraid that things might change. They never did, so I left it at that.'

Tommy took a long swig from his pint mug.

'So are they supporting you through college?'

'Partly. I get a grant, but still live with them during holidays – they're a bit like a new mum and dad I suppose.'

All of a sudden Tommy realised that unlike Marion, this girl seemed interested in him. Marion had never enquired about him or his family for that matter. She just talked about herself – what she did, what she liked, what she wanted and how she would get it.

He was silent for a while as he studied Paula a little more. He determined that she was actually very attractive, her masses of dark hair cascading down to her slim shoulders. Her tight ribbed jumper accentuating her shapely figure.

'So where are your family living?' he asked in an attempt to resurrect the conversation.

'We're a bit all over the place, actually. My dad works a lot in Sweden, near Stockholm, and occasionally in Belgium – Antwerp, so we have a small flat in each place. It's so much cheaper than hotels and an investment to boot. My mum does a lot of lecturing around Europe, so she quite often tags along with him. Our family home is near Sandwich in Kent. I just used to go wherever they were at the time.'

'Wow! That must be quite exciting for you. Gives you a chance to see places – I'd have loved something like that.'

'Well, it wasn't actually. They were always so wrapped up in their work that I felt lonely most of the time. My mum was rarely around and my dad would be at work or in his study, so it was pretty miserable. But I shouldn't complain because I wanted for nothing. They were quite generous that way.'

'Do you have any brothers or sisters?'

'No, I'm an only child as they say but I'm not spoiled rotten like some.'

'Sounds like we both suffered from the same problem though for entirely different reasons,' Tommy deduced.

'So have you met anyone since you arrived here?…I mean…'

'No, not yet,' she interrupted, 'you are the first guy I've really had a conversation with.'

'Great! So let's hope we can have lots more.' Tommy found himself saying. It just slipped out, he didn't intend to make such a forward remark so early on.

'Yeah, I'd like that,' she replied. 'Perhaps we can meet up again tomorrow after lectures?'

Tommy's heart was pounding again. But this time much more violently than that first time with Marion in the refectory. This girl mesmerised him. He looked across the room at Marion, still flirting with the rower, but he no longer cared what she was up to. David Benson was right, she was indeed the college bicycle. He cursed himself for not having fully recognised her type when they were in Ardingly. After all, he had enough evidence. He just hadn't wanted to accept it.

Paula interrupted his thoughts. 'Do you fancy another drink? I'll buy.'

'I'd love one,' he replied, 'but I'll get them.'

'No, I insist, we're both students and if we are going to see each other occasionally then it's only fair that I pay my way.'

Tommy didn't argue. He just hoped that her word 'occasionally' would turn out to be a little more often. She got up and wriggled her way through the crowd of people around the bar. Tommy watched her every move with interest. He had noticed that her complexion appeared almost Mediterranean and he decided he would tactfully ask her about her ancestry.

Paula threaded her way back from the bar, slowly so as not to spill the two drinks, and gently placed them on the table.

'You've obviously been on holiday somewhere nice recently.' he ventured.

'What makes you think that?'

'Well you're still quite tanned – obviously you are the type that can go brown very quickly in the sun.'

'Yes I do actually, but it's probably all due to my grandmother, she was Italian, from Rome, the daughter of a count or 'conte', as they say in Italy. I tend to take after her apparently.'

'Which side – your mother or father?'

'Mother – and my mum's father was French so my mother is half and half. She speaks both languages fluently too.'

Tommy was impressed. Her life and family were so very different from his own rather impoverished background.

The thought occurred to him that she might consider him too common to bother with. But on the contrary, she seemed fascinated by his simple life history and kept pumping him for information between sips of her cider.

Eventually, their glasses were empty and Tommy stood up.

'I've got some reading to do for tomorrow so I'll have to go. Shall I walk you over to your hall?'

'Actually, I'm living out,' she said, 'my dad thought it better to buy somewhere for the duration of my degree, then I can sell it to give me the chance of buying a house wherever I end up working. I've got two other students in the spare bedrooms paying rent so it works out quite cheap really.'

Tommy just stood there gawping. He was so far out of her realm, yet she was totally unpretentious about it.

'You'll have to invite me for dinner sometime then,' he joked, 'but don't worry, I eat anything.'

And before she could answer he added 'where shall we meet tomorrow?'

'Well, if you'd like dinner, I suppose it would have to be my place, but Deidre is cooking – it's her turn - and she's not so hot, but I can ask her to make enough for one more if you fancy it?'

Tommy fancied it all right.

1966

Contentment

Tommy's relationship with Paula was maturing rapidly and by the spring of 1966 he had moved into one of the bedrooms in her house. Not that he used it for anything other than study, as he was far more comfortable in the king-sized bed he shared with Paula in her own quarters.

Although they were studying the same subjects and saw each other virtually every hour of every day there was never a dull moment for they had so many common interests, never any major disagreements, just total harmony, love and affection. Tommy couldn't imagine a life any better than he was experiencing at that moment.

He no longer had thoughts of Marion. He had had it out with her several months before, after she had tried to get involved with him again. He'd not held back and had told her exactly what he thought of her. Furthermore, rather unnecessarily, he had relayed what the rest of the students thought of her too. She had cried for hours, and hidden herself away in her room for several days.

Eventually he became so worried that she might do something stupid that he went to her room to check she was all right, only to be told to clear off in a torrent of expletives. So he did, and he never let it bother him again.

That summer, Paula had invited him to spend some time with her parents in Kent. Little did he know that she was planning to use the visit to seek her parents' approval of Tommy as a possible future husband.

He was concerned about what they might think of his simple background but it never occurred to him that he was being vetted.

Much to his surprise, her parents were nothing like the picture he had conjured up in his mind. He had imagined a huge mansion of a property, a rather stern, slightly pompous disapproving father, full of his own importance. And a mother who had time for nothing but her work, delegating all her wifely duties to an imaginary cook, and housekeeper and being driven around by a chauffeur in a grey flannel suit and cap.

Nothing was further from the truth. Yes, the house was a spacious, architecturally designed home in Walmer, a couple of miles outside Sandwich, a short walk from the seafront, but not quite the mansion of Tommy's imagination. Paula's parents were as unassuming as they were engaging and accepted Tommy immediately. Paula was radiant with delight.

'So, you're both doing Biosciences then?' her father asked as they settled with their gin and tonics in the lounge before supper. 'Any idea what you plan to do with your degree when you've finished, Tommy?' he added.

Tommy leaned toward the coffee table and put down his drink. 'I'd really like to do something that would make a difference, something perhaps to improve or protect the environment.' he replied.

'Good man!' Paula's father said 'There's no shortage of opportunities in that sphere, though you won't make your fortune at it.'

'I'm not sure I want to make a fortune necessarily, after all, I'm not used to that, so I wouldn't actually miss it. What matters to me is doing something I enjoy.'

'Good man!' Paula's father said again.

'How about you Paula – what's your plan?'

'I'll do whatever Tommy does, go wherever Tommy goes, as long as we are together I don't care.' she replied.

'But you'll have a career?'

'Yes, of course.'

'Good girl!' he replied. Well, when you get your degrees, I'll see if I can help in any way, after all, I have lots of contacts, so too has your mother.'

'Yes Dad, I know - thanks.' Paula replied resignedly.

1969

Reward

Tommy and Paula were in their last term of University, awaiting their results. The graduation ceremony was just 4 weeks away.

They had both worked hard for their final papers, a task that was made all the easier by studying together, neither of them wanting to show less commitment.

Now they were waiting. Exams, theses and essays were over and they were discussing life after university.

Tommy thought a 'year out' might be good before they started their career.

Paula agreed, and suggested an expedition up the Amazon might be a fascinating if somewhat dangerous choice. So they started researching and planning for that, while they awaited their results.

'We'll need a lot of money, Paula,' Tommy said.

'Yeah, but my dad said that he would give me a thousand if I got a first, and I'm pretty sure I can achieve that.' Paula replied. 'Then we might be able to get some part time work somewhere.'

Tommy marvelled at her self-confidence. He just wished he could be as sure of himself.

A week later the results were out. Paula got her 'First, Tommy a 2/1. Both were cock-a-hoop.

And they booked their airfares.

1970

Disaster

On January 6th 1970, Tommy and Paula flew British Airways from Heathrow to Miami, Florida with five thousand pounds – a present from Paula's parents.

They planned to fly to Caracas in Venezuela, then after a circular tour of Georgetown in Guyana, Paramaribo in Suriname and Cayenne in French Guiana, they would arrive in Manaus in the heart of the Amazon rainforest.

This final destination, situated on the Negro River, was just eleven miles from the Amazon River itself, from where they were planning to hire a boat to explore the area.

Tommy and Paula arrived at Félix Eboué Airport in Cayenne, to find that their plane to Manaus had been cancelled due to a technical fault, the airline said. All later flights were fully booked over the week ahead.

'Well, we've got two choices,' Tommy suggested, 'we either book our flight for next week and stay here or we find another place to explore, and book a flight from there.'

Paula preferred the latter option.

But as they sat sipping their rum & cokes, an older, rather scruffily dressed, heavily built guy with a bushy moustache and steel grey hair gathered in a pony-tail, sitting at a table next to them, leaned over and in a mixture of French and poor English offered them an alternative.

'Je m'appelle Pierre. You want Manaus, Oui?' He asked.

'Oui!' Paula replied.

'J'ai un avion de transport qui part aujourd'hui. Je vous prendrai pour 10 dollars US chacun.'

Tommy's French was poor, so it was left with Paula to translate and finalise the transaction.

'He says he'll take us today for $10 each – he's apparently got a transport plane.'

Tommy looked the guy over, wondering whether he was trustworthy.

'Ask him what sort of plane it is,' Tommy suggested, 'and make sure it's got its airworthiness certificate or whatever.'

'Oui...Oui, je comprends, tout est bon - it's OK. - DC3 - très bons avions. Ils durent longtemps.' The guy replied.

Tommy looked at Paula who gave a slight nod of her head.

'OK,' said Tommy, 'Let's do it. What time do you leave?'

'I come for you 15.30, ici,' he replied stabbing the table with a nicotine-stained forefinger, whereupon he finished his glass of beer, picked up a small, tired looking canvas backpack from the floor under his table and walked off toward the toilets.

'Do you reckon he's legit?' Tommy asked. 'I mean, you don't think he's a drug-runner or anything like that, do you?'

'No idea,' Paula replied, 'but he didn't look dangerous or anything. There's lots of DC3's operating as transport planes in third world countries too, and they are reasonably reliable and easy to maintain, so it could be fine. I wonder what cargo he's got going to Manaus?'

'We'll soon see.' Tommy replied.

Sure enough, at 3.30 pm Pierre arrived, carrying no more than the same canvas backpack he had earlier.

'OK. We go now.'

Tommy and Paula followed him through the customs gate and out of the building. They walked across the apron to the red and silver DC3 parked near the maintenance hanger, 'Jungl'Air' in white lettering neatly painted down the side of the fuselage. The 'plane looked clean, as if freshly washed, which filled the pair with a little more confidence.

They climbed up the ladder and into the fuselage, filled to bursting point with pallets of unrecognisable goods wrapped in grey plastic film and covered with cargo nets.

'Les sièges sont dans le cockpit. Asseyez-vous s'il vous plait.'

The pair acknowledged, and took the co-pilot and navigator seats, which had clearly not been used for some time, as they were both covered in a sticky dust.

Pierre took the pilot seat and started the engines. After brief checks and a short conversation with the control tower, they taxied out to the airstrip.

And they were off and airborne on their four-hour journey.

Unfortunately, they never arrived at their destination. After leaving Cayenne, their plane disappeared off the radar some ninety minutes from Manaus.

Despite massive air searches along the route that the plane was understood to have taken and detailed aerial examination of areas where experts felt that the plane might have come down, no wreckage was ever found. Attempts at traversing the impenetrable jungle on foot proved fruitless and after 2 weeks of searching the teams were stood down.

Back in UK, the Snellings and the Dixons waited in vain for news of Tommy and Paula's adventure.

2008

Discovery

On the 9th July 2008, thirty eight years later, a team of loggers working in an area twenty miles south of Santarém discovered the vine and moss-laden wreckage of a twin-propped aircraft and adjacent to it, they uncovered a small grave with a gravestone made from an aircraft seat back. On it was scratched in the plastic just three words and a date:
'Pierre – Pilot. RIP 1972'
The largest part of the 'plane's virtually hidden fuselage appeared to have been lived in for some time, with beds made from tree branches and plastic from the palletised cargo. However, the cargo itself and parts from the aircraft cockpit were missing. Clearly there had been survivors.

Two weeks later, on the 25th July in the same year, the team of investigators searching for an unknown number of survivors stumbled into a collection of mud and timber huts in a clearing some six miles from the downed aircraft.
There, they found an indigenous tribe of 42 adults and 17 children and amongst them six white adults all answering to the surname 'Norton'.
Tommy Norton, now 61 and Paula Dixon aged 60, had survived the crash with only minor injuries but had been unable to find their way out of the jungle. The tribe of Indians with whom they were now living had eventually rescued them. Pierre had broken his leg in two places in the crash and though healed, had

been unable to walk. Rather than leave him, the couple had decided to stay with him at the aircraft until they were found. Pierre died two years later after being bitten by a pit viper.

Tommy and Paula had used the 'plane's cargo of rice and dried beans both to sustain themselves and to offer to the tribe as payment for their acceptance into their camp and their way of life.

Following their simple, tribal wedding, Paula had given birth to four children, three boys and a girl, all now in their thirties.

Paula's father, 82 in that year, never expecting to see his daughter again, flew to Caracas to meet up with the pair and his four grandchildren prior to their flight back to UK.

Tommy's guardians, Dr. and Mrs. Snelling died around ten years prior to his return, but in their wills had bequeathed everything they owned to Tommy, were he to be found.

Tommy and Paula are now officially married and currently working jointly with a number of Amazon conservation organisations. After 38 years living in the Amazon and their first hand knowledge of the Amazon tribal way of life, they are considered to be experts in their field.

Some months after their return, one of Tommy's university friends, who had read about their extraordinary story in the newspapers, made contact with Tommy. During their conversation, he mentioned that his old flame Marion Smythe had failed to attain her degree, had become jobless and unloved, an unmarried single mother of two and was apparently now alone and homeless in London - an alcoholic.

****

Other books by Tom Wyatt:

'**The Switch**' – A Thriller.
Danny Redmayne is a courier
Smuggling South African
diamonds from Amsterdam to
the London jewellery quarter.
He thinks he deserves a better
deal, so he decides to take a
run for himself but finds he
gets into more trouble than he
bargained for.
Jeff Blythe works for an oil

company in South Africa and through curiosity gets
caught up in the illegal diamonds trade. Danny and
Jeff's paths eventually cross with devastating
consequences.

Published on Amazon.

About the Author

Tom Wyatt worked in Engineering Construction
upon a number of projects in countries around the
world. He retired in 2004 and commenced writing
fiction a year later, based upon ideas developed from
his owns experiences and the people he'd met over
his working life. He lives with his family in Norfolk,
UK, a keen sailor, he spends his spare hours refitting
his old boat and constantly repairing his equally old
farm buildings.

Printed in Great Britain
by Amazon

59686944R00095